"Which house model do you like best?" Brady asked.

He glanced at Abby. "Come on. Stop worrying and get happy. This is supposed to be the part where you get all excited and make me feel like a hero."

Her mouth lifted slightly at his silliness, and he felt better.

"I love that one," she said, pointing at the plans.

"The country cottage?" He'd chosen that one for her the minute he'd seen it. It was simple and charming. Like her. "Look at the interior plan, too. We can change it if you like, but it's perfect for your daughter's needs."

She looked up at him with those soft brown eyes. His chest expanded. She liked it. She liked it a lot. He realized then that he'd been overanxious about this home makeover, afraid she'd regret letting him barge into her life and turn it upside down.

"You think of everything, don't you?" she said, smiling.

That was the reaction he'd been looking for.

Linda Goodnight, a *New York Times* bestselling author and winner of a RITA® Award in inspirational fiction, has appeared on the Christian bestseller list. Her novels have been translated into more than a dozen languages. Active in orphan ministry, Linda enjoys writing fiction that carries a message of hope in a sometimes dark world. She and her husband live in Oklahoma. Visit her website, lindagoodnight.com, for more information.

Books by Linda Goodnight

Love Inspired

The Buchanons

Cowboy Under the Mistletoe
The Christmas Family

Whisper Falls

Rancher's Refuge
Baby in His Arms
Sugarplum Homecoming
The Lawman's Honor

Redemption River

Finding Her Way Home
The Wedding Garden
A Place to Belong
The Christmas Child
The Last Bridge Home

Visit the Author Profile page at Harlequin.com for more titles.

The Christmas Family

New York Times Bestselling Author

Linda Goodnight

HARLEQUIN® LOVE INSPIRED®

Recycling programs
for this product may
not exist in your area.

LOVE INSPIRED BOOKS

ISBN-13: 978-0-373-87993-9

The Christmas Family

For everyone to whom much is given,
from him much will be required...
—*Luke* 12:48

For my Aunt Edith, last of the Porter dynasty. Ninety looks good on you! Thank you for always being proud of me. Love you, dear lady.

Chapter One

Brady Buchanon had planned his escape well. Three more minutes and he was out of here for the day.

He hurriedly tossed his tools into the back of the work truck, eager to be gone. Man, he loved this time of year! Cool, crisp and clear weather, and Christmas practically dripped from the trees.

He clicked the locks on his royal blue F-350, waited for Dawg, his faithful mutt to leap into the seat and was about to climb inside himself when his father, owner of Buchanon Built Construction Company and, by all rights, Brady's boss, stepped out into the late November day.

"Brady, hold up."

Not fast enough. Brady blew out a resigned breath. He leaned a hand on the truck top and waited, though not at all patiently.

"Been meaning to talk to you about something."

"Sure. What's up?"

"This makeover thing you do every Christmas, better cancel this year."

The request sailed right over Brady's head. "Too late. I already have the recipient lined up."

Dan Buchanon, his salt-and-pepper hair hidden under a

Buchanon Built ball cap, scratched at the side of his neck. "You've made the announcement?"

"On my way there now. Dad, you should see this house. It's bad, but Buchanon Built can make it shine." Donating a home makeover for one needy family each Christmas was Brady's favorite event of the year, and the publicity was great for business, an important consideration to his father.

"I appreciate the sentiment, son, and in years past didn't mind the lost time and expense but not this year. We need all hands on deck."

"I can work it out. Don't worry. Buchanon projects won't suffer. The guys who volunteer can work on the makeover on their downtime or when things are slow."

But Dan was shaking his head. "With all the work on the schedule and the slowdowns we've encountered, you don't have time for charity. *We* don't have time for charity. Jaylee just told me you still don't have a plumber lined up for the Edwards project."

"I'm working on it."

Irritation flashed on Dan's face. "And you want to pull off six paying jobs for a freebie? Forget it, Brady. Forget it. And fix the plumber problem today. No more delays. No more excuses."

Brady's blood heated. He held his temper in check better these days, but no one worked him up like his dad. And vice versa. "I'm doing my best."

His father's thick jaw clenched. "I don't want your best. I want the problem solved."

"It's not as if I haven't tried." Leaving the truck door open and the dog in the seat, Brady pushed away from the vehicle to face his father. He spread his hands in a plea. "Be reasonable, Dad." Like that was going to happen in this lifetime. "Jack Taylor had a heart attack. The man can't work." And the plumbing problem had nothing to do with Brady's home makeover.

"Then get someone else."

Brady didn't believe in kicking a man when he was down. "Jack's business needs the work. And he's the best plumber around."

"And *we* need to bring this project in on time or lose a boatload of money. The vandals have thrown us behind on everything and now subcontractors decide not to show up. Buchanon Construction was built on dependability and speed. If Jack can't work, find someone who can. Spend your time on business, not on some feel-good Christmas project."

Brady stifled an angry retort. He had places to go and much more enjoyable things to do tonight than get into another fight with his father. A plumber who'd had a heart attack didn't "decide" not to work. The choice was out of the man's hands.

"I'll talk to Jack's wife first thing in the morning." Mary Taylor was busting tail trying to keep the small plumbing business going while taking care of her ailing husband. Good plumbing temps were hard to come by. He should know. He'd called plenty, though telling that to his father was a waste of good clean Texas air.

"Tomorrow isn't good enough." Dan stacked his hands on his hips for emphasis. "I want plumbers on the job site by six in the morning to fix the problem." He jabbed a finger toward Brady. "See her now. Tonight. And don't take no for an answer. Understood?"

Brady took a step back, fuming, his back teeth tight enough to crack.

"Right. Sure. The job will get done." Brady always did the job, but his father seldom noticed progress. He only noticed the problems.

As if his demands were law—which they sort of were— Dan spun away and slammed the office door behind him. The sound reverberated in the formerly pleasant evening.

Adrenaline jacked to ninety, Brady dragged a frustrated hand down his face. Another minute and he would have been gone. Another minute and he could have gone through an entire work shift without letting his father get under his skin.

He was six inches taller and fifty pounds heavier than Dan Buchanon and had been the foreman at Buchanon Built since graduating Texas Tech eight years ago, but his father still managed to make him feel as insignificant as sawdust.

Brady turned back to the truck, where Dawg sat behind the wheel as if he was about to drive away. The comical picture erased some of Brady's frustration. "You driving?"

"Can't. He doesn't have a license."

Brady pivoted toward the voice. Dawson, one of Brady's three brothers and the dimpled twin to Sawyer, ambled around the end of the warehouse, tool belt bouncing against his hip like a gunslinger.

"Don't let Dad ruin your day. He's been in a meeting with Marilyn Tenbears for the last hour and a half."

"That explains it."

Marilyn Tenbears owned a strip of woods along Gratitude Creek that Dad was determined to purchase. Marilyn was just as determined to either get rich from the sale or keep the land.

"He thinks I should shelve the makeover."

Dawson unhooked his tool belt. "I heard. But weren't you planning to tell the recipient tonight that her home had been chosen for the remodel?"

"Still am. In fact, I'm heading over there now. Want to come along?"

"You're still going to do it?"

"That's the plan."

Dawson cast a concerned glance toward the office door. "What about Dad? How will you get this past him?"

"I'll think of something. He'll come around."

"He doesn't like his orders to be ignored."

"Dad never likes anything I do, but I get the work done."

"That's because Buchanon Built has flourished with you as foreman in a way it never could with Dad in the role. He was too harsh with subcontractors."

Brady huffed. "No kidding? Dad? Harsh?"

The brothers exchanged a chuckle.

"Hop in, Dawson, my man." Brady popped a palm against the roof of his truck and slid into the driver's seat. "Santa Claus is about to do his thing."

"What about the plumber?"

"I'll worry about him later."

With an amused shake of his head, Dawson shucked his tool belt and climbed into the big Ford with his brother, relegated Dawg to the backseat, and slammed the door. "No wonder you and Dad butt heads. Who is this year's beneficiary of a Buchanon Built makeover?"

"Abby Webster. You know who she is. She works at the Buttered Biscuit."

"Yeah." Dawson turned an interested face toward Brady. "I know who you mean. Good waitress, all business and not too smiley or talkative but remembers exactly how I like my eggs and coffee." He put the edge of his hand at nose level. "Up to here, pretty tall with long brown hair she wears in a ponytail over her shoulder. Right?"

Brady glanced from the road to his brother. "Tall? She's not tall."

"Compared to you she's not tall. Compared to other women she is."

Brady conceded a truth he had to live with and really didn't mind all that much. He was some kind of genetic throwback to his giant Celtic ancestors, both in looks and size. Even his rust-brown hair, which he clipped short, was out of sync with the rest of the family. Dawson, on the other hand, was so black-hair-and-blue-eyed pretty, he belonged on the cover of a magazine. Not that Brady would tell his manly little brother he thought he was pretty.

"Did you know she has a little girl with some kind of handicap?"

"Like I said, Abby Webster's not much of a talker. Brings my food and skitters away." From the backseat, the dog poked a cold nose in Dawson's neck. Dawson gave him a gentle shove. "Stay in the back, fella."

"Wait until you see this place, Dawson." The enthusiasm Brady had for the Christmas project bubbled up inside him. "Abby and her little girl need this makeover badly. The house is run-down, shingles missing, windows cracked, no handicap accessibility. She's going to be thrilled."

"How do you find out this stuff?"

"I ask. I look." Truth was, he drove all over town looking at houses. "People tell me."

"That's because they know you're a soft touch like Mom."

"To whom much is given, much is required."

"That's Mom's favorite verse."

"Yeah, well, she's right. Giving back is the right thing to do, and it feels pretty good, too, especially at Christmas." And nothing made him feel as worthwhile and as necessary to the planet, especially after a run-in with his critical father. "I'm not backing out no matter what Dad thinks."

"What if he pulls the powerful Buchanon rug out from under the project? You need the company to make this happen."

Brady hadn't had time to think that far, but he couldn't deny the possibility. When Dad was crossed, he could be a tough customer.

But Brady had made up his mind. One way or the other, Abby Webster was getting a home makeover. And he couldn't wait to see how happy she was when she heard the news.

* * *

Gabriel's Crossing, Texas, was the kind of place where few people crossed the railroad tracks into "that" part of town unless they lived there.

Abby Webster and her daughter lived there.

Legs aching from the twelve-hour shift at the Buttered Biscuit and delighted to be heading home, Abby encouraged her exhausted old CR-V to travel the distance from the Huckleberry Play School to the sagging house on Cedar Corner. Anyone could find her house without the number—something that had been missing far longer than Abby had lived there. Hers was the house with duct tape over a crack in the front window and the cheery crayon drawings of blue and red angels hanging next to the crack. Her four-year-old had a thing for colorful angels.

Abby parked in the driveway, a strip of blacktop with dead grass poking through the cracks. "Out you go, jelly fingers."

Her daughter, the joy of her life, giggled from her car seat. "I'm hungry."

"Imagine that, Lila Webster is hungry." Abby hopped out of the car and went around to the other side. She opened the door and unbuckled her daughter's seat belt. "How about a peanut butter and broccoli sandwich?"

"Ew, Mommy."

Smiling into her child's chocolate-colored eyes, Abby lifted the four-year-old into her arms, thankful Lila was still small. Hopefully, by the time Lila was too big to carry, they could afford a house with the space for her special equipment. Or just maybe Lila would be walking on her own without a walker or wheelchair. Such possibilities existed and Abby would never give up hope that the mild function in her child's spinal cord would continue to develop.

"Okay, then, maybe macaroni and raisins?"

Lila cocked her head, a tiny frown between dark eyebrows as she considered the combination. Then, her face lit with enthusiasm, she said, "Okay!"

Marveling at the precious gift of her child, Abby juggled Lila and her keys to unlock the front door and bump it open with her hip. Raising a child with special needs wasn't easy, but Lila's undaunted spirit and joy in living made everything worthwhile. What other child would react with such pleasure to a meal of macaroni and raisins?

"Were you a good girl at school today?"

"Yeth."

"Did Gerry say mean things to you?"

"He was nice."

Abby breathed a sigh of relief. Some kids didn't understand why Lila was different. While most didn't seem to mind that Lila wore braces and didn't walk normally, some were downright cruel at times.

Dropping her keys on the table, Abby set her daughter on the love seat with the ever-present crayons and paper and went to the kitchen to create another macaroni masterpiece.

The pasta was on to boil when Lila called, "Somebody's here, Mom. In a big, big car."

Abby heard the rumble of an engine and identified the big, big car as most likely a truck. Hmm. She hadn't ordered anything through UPS.

"Not expecting guests." She went to the side window and peeked out at the graying evening. A bright blue pickup had pulled into the driveway behind her Honda. "Who in the world is that?"

Lila, busy with another of her art projects, didn't look up. "I don't know. Maybe Santa Claus."

Abby smiled, though the statement squeezed her chest. This year was the first time Lila was old enough to really get into the idea of Santa Claus, but Lila's medical expenses kept their small budget strained to the breaking point. Lila wouldn't notice the small size of the Christmas gifts under the tree, but her mother would.

"Too early for Santa, so I don't know who…" Her voice dwindled away as two gorgeous males exited the gleaming blue truck and sauntered up her drive. They looked familiar and they had to be brothers. Though one was half a foot taller than the other, their strides matched and they swung their arms with identical confidence as though the world was their oyster. With looks like those, it probably was.

"Oh, my." As they came closer, she recognized them. Buchanons, two of the four sear-your-eyeballs-gorgeous brothers.

Abby opened the front door as the men stepped upon her wooden porch. A weak board groaned and she held her breath, hoping they wouldn't fall through.

"I don't have home owners' insurance," she blurted.

The taller one with swimming-pool eyes tilted his head. She wished she could remember his name. "Ma'am?"

"The porch," she managed, feeling stupider by the minute as her brain refused to work but her mouth kept going. "Some of the boards are weak. You're big. Don't fall through."

Both men dipped their heads to stare at the porch and then exchanged glances. "Needs work."

"Don't I know it," Abby said.

She stood in the doorway, blocking the entrance and wishing they'd state their business. Buchanons didn't exactly hang out on this side of town and they were letting out expensive heat.

"That's what we want to talk to you about."

"My porch?" Abby poked a finger into her breastbone and then flung out her hand. "Sorry, I can't afford to hire anyone right now."

"Oh, no, that's not why we're here," said Mr. Swimming-

Pool Eyes. "I'm Brady Buchanon and this is my brother, Dawson. Buchanon Built Construction."

Brady and Dawson. She could never remember one brother from the other, only that all four were heartthrobs. She did, however, remember their routine orders at the diner.

Two gorgeous men on her doorstep was not the norm and she was pedaling fast to figure out why they were here. She pointed to Dawson. "Eggs over easy. And you—" Her finger went to Brady. "French toast and large milk but occasionally the house special."

A killer smile split Brady Buchanon's face. "You're making me hungry."

"Hazard of the job. I equate everyone in Gabriel's Crossing with their most common order at the café." Which, now that she thought about it, wasn't too flattering.

"May we come in for a minute?" Brady asked. "We'd like to talk to you about something."

"Oh. Well, sure, I guess so." She stepped to one side. "Come on in. Just be careful—"

Brady gave her another of those swoon-worthy grins. "We'll try not to break the floor."

"I'm sorry, I didn't mean that as insult. It's just this house is—"

He waved her off. "Don't worry about it. I'm a big boy."

"You certainly are." A hot blush raced up her neck and heated her cheeks. Her mouth was out of control tonight. At five-nine, she was unused to having men tower over her. And Brady Buchanon definitely towered. "Have a seat. That little sprite on the couch is Lila."

Lila had been staring at the men with the wide-eyed curiosity of a preschooler.

"Pretty picture," Brady said as he lowered his oversize frame onto the faded blue sofa next to Lila. Dawson took the only chair in the room, leaving Abby to perch on the other side of Lila. The couch was fuller than it had ever been.

"I'm making a kiss-mas twee. See? That's an angel."

Brady studied the crayon drawing earnestly. "Almost as pretty as you."

"Want to color with me?"

If the man had a heart, those brown eyes would melt it.

"Maybe next time, okay? Do you mind if I talk to your mommy for a few minutes?"

Lila shrugged and scribbled a little harder on her kiss-mas tree. "Okay."

Brady gazed over the top of Lila's head at Abby. "I don't know if you're familiar with my family's business, Buchanon Built Construction—"

"I am." Was he joking? The Buchanons practically owned Gabriel's Crossing. You couldn't live in this town without seeing one of their white trucks with the big blue logo or passing a sign that announced a Buchanon Built home.

"Great. Every year our company offers a home makeover to someone in town."

"I've heard about that. Last year, you remodeled Ted Bickford's house and built an addition to make room for all their children."

Ted and Teresa were kid magnets who had adopted six and fostered as many more on any given day. The people were saints.

Brady beamed as though she'd awarded him the jackpot prize. "That's right. We did. Nice family."

But what did that have to do with her? "Excuse me a sec, will you? I have macaroni on the stove." And she hoped it hadn't boiled to mush.

"I like macaroni," Lila said, looking up. "With raisins."

Abby laughed a little as she hurried the few steps to the kitchen to drain the pasta. The kitchen-dining area was small, a throwback to the days when microwaves and dishwashers were unheard-of. "Lila would eat rocks if I added macaroni."

She turned to reenter the living room only to discover that Brady had followed and now blocked the narrow doorway, as large and intimidating and every bit as beautiful as some mythological warrior. Her pulse did a double step.

Whoa, what was that all about?

"My niece and nephew are the same way." He stepped aside, letting her pass, a movement that brought them in very close contact. Her shoulder brushed his arm. He smelled good, like new wood and Eternity cologne. "Mom cooks T-bone steaks and the kids want macaroni."

Disconcerted by the highly unusual skitter of pulse and the hum of blood in her veins, Abby hurried back to the couch. Brady followed, but not before he'd casually leaned in to the kitchen and had a look around.

What was he doing? If she didn't know him by reputation, she'd think he was casing the place for robbery. Or worse.

"Macaroni rocks the world, right, Lila?" said Dawson, whom she'd dubbed the thoughtful one long ago at the café.

"Uh-huh." Lila went right back to coloring. This time the angel was yellow.

"Now, as I was saying," Brady said, retaking his place at the end of the couch. He leaned forward, startling blue eyes holding hers and his big hands clasped in front of him. "We offer a home makeover every Christmas. This year, we'd like to remodel *your* house. Merry Christmas, Abby."

His big white smile was dazzling, and she understood he expected her to be thrilled.

She wasn't. She was embarrassed. Mortified. Humiliation heated her cheeks to chili-pepper status.

She had flashbacks to pitying teachers dragging used shoes and coats from school closets.

Her back stiffened. "That's very nice of you, but no. I couldn't accept."

Brady's smile disappeared. "No?"

"No. But thank you for the offer." She stood, expecting him to leave.

The brothers exchanged looks. They were good at that. Must be some kind of sibling symbiosis, although she wouldn't know. Being a street kid who had never even known her mother, Abby had grown up alone, mostly in group homes. Not that she minded so much now that she was an independent adult. What doesn't kill you makes you stronger. She was happy on her own. Truly, she was. She had Lila and a job and this house. She most definitely was not a charity case.

And the fact that she'd all but swooned over the handsome Buchanon brothers humiliated her even more. Men like them didn't look twice at a girl like her.

Even her ears were burning now. She wanted to dissolve right into the floor of her run-down, makeover-worthy old house.

"If you're worried we would interfere with your everyday living, we won't. We'll work out a schedule that fits yours."

Abby swallowed, her pride throbbing like an ingrown toenail. The house needed repairs but she'd get to them eventually without becoming the object of someone's pity. "Lila and I are doing fine the way we are."

"If you're worried about the money, this is a gift. No charge."

Which made it even worse. "I pay my own way, Mr. Buchanon."

Brady stared at her as if her brain was as loose as the boards on her porch. Finally, he nodded and slowly rose.

"Sorry to have bothered you." He looked so disappointed she almost caved and said yes. In fact, if her pride wasn't so insulted, she would agree anyway, just to see him smile again.

"No bother. I'm sure there are others far needier than Lila and I."

The brothers did that glancing thing again. Brady took a business card from his pocket and handed it to her. "In case you change your mind, my number is on here. Call me anytime."

"Thanks." Her smile was brittle. "See you at the Buttered Biscuit."

"Mister," Lila said, though it sounded more like "misser."

"I drawed this for you." She offered the yellow angel to him. "Hang it on your window."

His face softened. "It's beautiful. Thank you, Lila."

Lila beamed at him, pleased with herself and proud of her scrawling, four-year-old jumble of lines, circles and color.

Some of the starch went out of Abby's spine at the exchange between her small child and the giant man who accepted the drawing as if it was as valuable as a van Gogh.

Brady Buchanon was a nice guy. A guy who could easily get to her.

All the more reason to refuse his offer.

Chapter Two

"That was different," Dawson said as the brothers joined Dawg back inside the pickup.

Different didn't even come close to explaining the past ten minutes.

Stunned to numbness, Brady leaned over the steering wheel and stared at Abby Webster's house. The paint was peeling, the porch sagged—at least to his expert eye—and a dozen or more shingles were missing from the roof. The inside was as retro as any he'd seen in a while. A child like Lila would never be able to maneuver a wheelchair or a walker through those narrow doors and hallways.

"No one's ever turned us down before."

"Kind of painful, wasn't it?" Dawson gave an exaggerated shudder.

"Why? I don't get it?" Brady flopped back against the seat cushion. "The house is in sad repair and she needs us. She *needs* us."

"Getting a little overwrought, aren't you, brother? Wounded pride, maybe?"

"Yeah!" Brady cranked the engine, listened to the rumble and put the shifter in gear. "She's supposed to be thrilled."

"Wonder why she refused. Do you think she actually doesn't see the problems?"

"Nah, it's not that. She was upset, not oblivious. The problem is, I don't know what button we pushed to fix it, but she was offended."

"The little girl was cute, huh?"

"Adorable." The truck bumped across the railroad tracks. The sun was in midset, shooting orange fingers through a purple sky. "Did you notice her artwork all over the walls?"

"Couldn't miss it. The mom's not too bad, either."

Brady gave him a hard look. "What's that supposed to mean?"

"They need this remodel. Maybe you could turn on the Buchanon charm."

Brady snorted. "No."

"You haven't dated anyone since Kiley and that was months ago."

"Not interested. I'm a builder, not a Romeo." Never mind the strange sensation that had tingled up his arms when Abby brushed past him in the kitchen. Or the weird, *weird* heat in his chest when Lila gave him her angel drawing. "You're the man about town. You ask her out."

"The Christmas makeover is your project." Dawson's wide shoulders lifted in a shrug. "We can always find another recipient. That side of town has plenty of candidates."

"Yeah, I suppose you're right. Plan B." But Abby and her little girl needed the remodel more than anyone else he'd considered. Lila, especially, according to his sources at the day care, suffered from the lack of special-needs accessories in her home. He wanted to do *that* makeover.

The next morning Brady awakened hungry. Nothing unusual about that, but this morning he decided to eat breakfast at the Buttered Biscuit. Call him stubborn or perverse, but he wasn't ready to give up on Miss Abby Webster. If a little of his presence reminded her of how much she needed him and what a good guy he was, all the better.

The drive to the café took a few minutes. He'd built his house, or rather half of it, on the edge of town not far from the river in a copse of bald cypress and red oak. As he liked to say, his home was a work in progress. The lower floor was finished and the rest evolved in squeezed-out hours and minutes. All of the Buchanon kids except Quinn had, over time, acquired a Buchanon Built home.

Older brother Quinn was, himself, a work in progress, still trying to pull his act together after a life-altering accident, though most of the family thought ten years was enough time for anyone. Forgiving Jake Hamilton, the cause of the accident, had made a difference, but Quinn had a ways to go.

Brady turned the lock on his front door and whistled his way out into the cool morning with Dawg at his heel.

As he drove into town and down First Street to the café, gray fog crawled along the ground in mysterious wisps and wiggles.

"Sit tight, pal, and I'll bring you a sausage patty." Brady gave Dawg a pat and rolled the window down enough for the animal to stick his nose out if the mood struck. Dawg, accustomed to waiting for his master, put his chin on his paws and went to sleep.

Breakfast smells hit Brady full in the olfactory glands the minute he entered the café. His stomach reacted with wild abandon.

As usual this early in the morning, the café was jammed and the clatter of conversations mixed with the clink of plates and the cook's voice calling "order up!"

An old-time diner-style café that served up home cooking and comfort food, the Buttered Biscuit was the place to be for good eats and all the latest and greatest in Gabriel's Crossing news.

Brady greeted friends and acquaintances as he made his way to a table still cluttered with someone else's empty plates and took a seat.

Jan, the owner and baker of the fluffiest biscuits in Texas, whipped past. "Get that in a sec, Brady."

"No rush." Which wasn't technically true. He was always in a rush these days.

Two other waitresses were on duty, all of them moving at Mach speed to fill cups and deliver plates. Abby Webster, pad in hand, took orders two tables away. She looked up, spotted Brady and hesitated as if she didn't want to see him.

Too bad.

She had kept him up late trying to figure out why anyone would refuse a free home makeover from the best builders in the area. The least she could do was bring him a cup of coffee.

She whipped toward him and he noticed her as he never had before, though he ate at the diner fairly often. Probably because, as Dawson said, she was all business. The other waitresses smiled and bantered with the customers—he noticed *them*—but Abby simply worked. He wondered, randomly, if she did anything for fun.

"French toast and milk?" she asked. Her cheekbones were tipped in pink.

"Sure. And the strongest cup of coffee you have." Coffee, like her eyes. Dark and shiny and able to deliver a jolt.

She didn't offer a joke, as Jan would have, by asking him if he'd been out all night partying or some other sassmouthed comment she was known for. Abby simply scribbled his order, grabbed a pile of plates and sailed away.

He watched her move through the customers, topping off coffee and delivering checks as she made her way to the kitchen with his order.

She was actually kind of pretty, a truth that surprised

him this morning. Mink-colored hair that gleamed over one shoulder, huge dark eyes framed by thick, arching eyebrows and a wide, full mouth. On anyone else, the large features would be too much, but they looked good on her.

"What are you staring at, big brother?" Dawson pulled out the chair opposite him. Sawyer, the other twin, joined him on the right.

Brady ignored the question. "What are you two doing here?"

"Same as you. Too lazy to cook breakfast. Have you been able to locate a plumber for the Edwards job?"

Brady slapped the heel of one hand to his forehead. "Ah, man, I forgot."

He'd been so keyed up after the strange meeting with Abby he'd not given the plumber another thought until this moment.

"Dad's not going to be happy."

"I'll find someone." But not before the already-passed deadline of six o'clock. "Any ideas."

"A couple. You might call Richie Clonts up in Idabel."

"Good idea."

"Give Charity a call. She'll know his number."

Charity was their oldest sister, a powerhouse real estate agent with a steel-trap mind and a list of contacts a mile long.

He fished his cell phone from his hip pocket, got the number from his sister and called the plumber. Five minutes later, he hung up a happier man. "Richie can send someone tomorrow. Dad wanted someone today, but tomorrow is better than nothing."

Abby appeared with his coffee in a thick white mug and took orders from the twins.

"You're pretty busy," Sawyer said, saying the obvious with a toothy smile. Brady's younger brothers, especially Sawyer, were always scoping the field for ladies.

"Slammed, but it's letting up."

"Still have my phone number?" Brady asked.

Her gaze flicked his direction. She got pink again. "Haven't you chosen someone else?"

"I'd rather give you time to think about the offer."

"Why?"

The question caught Brady off guard, but he said, "I like your little girl and I can give her something she needs."

A look, almost of panic, flamed in Abby's eyes. Again, Brady wondered what her problem was.

"Lila and I are okay, but thanks. Anything else on these orders?"

The twins lifted their fingers off the table in an identical gesture. "We're good."

And Abby whirled away, leaving the Buchanon brothers staring after her.

"Stubborn," Brady muttered as he reached for the steaming cup.

"Embarrassed," Dawson said. "Did you see how she blushed?" Intuitive and empathetic, Dawson was the brother who always noticed things like that.

"Nah," Sawyer said, and laughed. "She was overwhelmed by my charm. Girls always turn pink in my studly presence."

His brothers hooted.

"Dawg's more charming than you."

"Prettier, too."

"Aw, thanks, guys." Sawyer hung his head in mock offense.

"Kidding aside, do you think we embarrassed her?" Brady asked.

"What's this *we* business? You're the guilty party."

The concept gave Brady pause. He'd never purposely embarrass someone, but maybe Dawson was right. Maybe Abby somehow mistook his intentions. Maybe she thought he was putting her down.

Man, he'd never considered such a thing.

"I think I should talk to her again, show her the possibilities."

The twins exchanged looks. "Can't take no for an answer, can you, Brady?"

Never had. Never would. Not when someone needed him, and he was convinced Abby and Lila needed his help.

Before he left, Brady slid a twenty-dollar bill under his plate.

He'd left her twenty dollars. Abby didn't know whether to be pathetically grateful or even more humiliated than she'd been last night.

"Wow, girlfriend, you must have been on your game this morning. Twenty bucks," Charla Patterson, one of the other waitresses and Abby's friend said as she helped clear the Buchanon table. "Have you caught the eye of one of Gabriel's Crossing's most eligible bachelors?"

Abby shook her head at the ridiculous notion. "Like that would ever happen."

"Hey, don't sell yourself short. You have lots to offer."

"Tell that to Warren." She'd trusted her ex-boyfriend, a man who'd promised love and marriage but bolted when he learned the child Abby carried would be special-needs. Now, she only felt loathing for the man who had never once laid eyes on his beautiful daughter.

"Warren was a user. It's time for you to stop beating yourself up over him and move on."

"I'm not beating myself up. I'm glad he's out of our lives."

"And I'm thankful for that. I never liked the guy, even though I still think you should force him to pay child support. You could use the money."

"No way. I don't want him involved with Lila any more than he wants to be. He doesn't deserve to be part of her life. Him or his lovely wife." She sounded bitter and didn't want to be. But his cruel rejection had stabbed deep and left her uncertain and bruised.

"There are good guys out there, hon. Guys like Brady Buchanon. His cute twin brothers, too."

A funny little twitter went off in Abby's belly. She clattered a fork onto a plate and ignored the feeling. "I have Lila. She's all I need."

"So why did Brady leave such a fat tip this morning?"

"Not because he's after me, that's for sure." She forced a laugh, surprised to be bothered by that truth. "Remember how the Buchanons give away a home makeover every Christmas?"

"Sure. The makeover is a big deal. A really big deal." Charla slapped a bleach rag against the tabletop as her eyes widened. "You don't mean—"

"Brady offered it to me."

"Abby! That's amazing. Congratulations. No one deserves a new home more than you."

"I turned him down."

"What? Are you out of your mind?"

"I don't need their help, Char. I can take care of my daughter and my house and my *life* without anyone."

"Oh, Abby." Charla looked at her with sympathy. Dishes rattled as they stacked them on the cart. "Sometimes you're too independent for your own good. Warren really did a number on you."

Warren wasn't the only one though, admittedly, he'd been the latest in bad decisions that had come back to bite her. Abby was smart enough to know her background made her wary. Nobody did something for nothing. Stick your heart out there and it would get tromped. Every time. If trying to fit into a family and failing at age thirteen hadn't proved that, Warren had.

Big, beautiful Brady Buchanon would have to find someone else to feel sorry for.

She stuck his twenty dollars into her pocket and debated on giving it back.

Lila's play school telephoned an hour before Abby's shift ended.

"For you, Abby," Jan called, holding her hand over the mouthpiece. "Christina at the play school."

The café was in the lull shortly before dinner hour and Abby was in the middle of filling and wiping down saltshakers. She recapped the latest one and went to the phone.

"Sorry," she said to Jan. "I'm out of minutes for my phone." But with Christmas coming, she was holding off on the purchase as long as possible.

"You know I don't care when it's important." Her boss, a sturdy, energetic woman with close-cropped blond waves, winked. "Lila's always important."

"Thanks, Jan." Her boss was good to her so Abby never wanted to take advantage. She took the phone and said, "Hello."

A minute later she hung up. "Jan, Lila had a bathroom accident at school. I really have to go over there, but I'll come back as soon as I take care of her."

Jan glanced around the quiet café. "Charla and I can handle it for an hour until Mercy gets here. Get Lila and go on home. Tell her accidents happen to everyone."

But they happened to Lila more than most. While her potty training had progressed to a good schedule considering the nerve damage below the waist, on occasion she had an accident.

Abby didn't know whether to be grateful for her boss's understanding or worried. She needed the hour on her paycheck, but Lila came first. "I'll see you at five-thirty in the morning then?"

"Deal." Jan waved her off.

The streets of Gabriel's Crossing bustled with Christmas preparations. City workers in cherry pickers were draping strands of green lighted garland from one side of First Street to the other. In the center of each garland was a huge green wreath with artificial candles and a big red bow.

Just looking at the decorations going up everywhere filled her with excited dread. She loved seeing Lila's excitement but wished she could give her more. Lila didn't even have grandparents or other relatives to spoil her and buy her things.

But that was okay. They didn't need anyone else. They had each other.

She swung by the house to pick up a change of clothes and reached Huckleberry Play School soon thereafter.

Greeted by Christina, the owner/operator of the day care where Lila had gone for the past year, Abby fretted. One of the rules of this facility was that children had to be potty trained. The staff accommodated Lila's special needs in other ways, but this was a rule for all children, not just Lila.

"I'm really sorry about this, Christina. Lila's been doing so well."

"She has. Don't worry about it this time, but if she regresses, we'll need to talk again."

"I understand." Truly she did, but this was the only preschool in town that accommodated Abby's long hours and odd work days. Plus, Lila loved it here. Abby wasn't sure what she would do if she had to find another placement.

"Lila is waiting in my office," Christina said. "She was very upset."

Abby hurried to the office and found her red-eyed daughter sitting with her small legs dangling from an adult chair. Chin on her chest, mouth tilted down, Lila was the picture of dejection.

Abby's heart broke at the sight. Her chest clutched as she gathered her child into her arms. "Hey, jelly fingers. Mom's here, and I brought your favorite outfit to change into."

"My jammies?" Lila asked hopefully.

Around a lump in her throat, Abby managed a chuckle. "We'll get into those after a bath at home. Okay? For now, how about your pink princess set?"

Lila sniffed, long and shuddery, and nodded her head.

Abby gathered her child into her arms and carried her to the bathroom to change, and then they headed home.

The usually chatty Lila said little in the car, though Abby tried to start distracting conversations about Christmas.

"Lila," Abby said, as they pulled into the blacktop drive and parked. "Accidents happen. Miss Jan said to remind you of that. You're doing great, and I'm proud of you."

"Will I ever be big like other kids?"

Unexpected tears jammed the back of Abby's nose and throat. She'd been dealing with the effects of Lila's mild spina bifida for years, but, instead of getting easier as Lila grew old enough to notice the world around her, the task became harder.

"You will always be the most awesome Lila in the world."

For now, this was enough to bring the faintest glimmer of a smile to her daughter's face. But how long before a nonanswer was not enough?

Heart heavy, Abby gathered her child into her arms and started to the house. As she stepped up on the porch, keys in one hand and Lila on her hip, the board she'd warned Brady Buchanon about gave way.

Her foot caught in the broken board and Abby struggled to maintain her balance. Struggled and failed. Instinctively trying to protect Lila, she twisted to the left and tumbled onto the porch in a heap. She lost her grip, and Lila hit the wooden porch and started to cry.

"Are you hurt? Oh, baby. You're okay. You're okay." In a panic, Abby scrambled to her feet and pulled Lila into her arms, searching for blood or bruises. With her nerve impairment, Lila didn't always know when she was injured.

Once she was certain no real emergency existed, Abby opened the door and carried Lila inside the living room. Both of them were shaking. She had never dropped her daughter. Never.

Lila curled up on the couch and sniveled. This hadn't been her best day.

Abby scooted onto the couch beside her daughter and laid her head against Lila's. "I'm sorry, baby. Do you hurt anyplace?"

"Uh-uh. Can I have a drink?" The usually sunny child sounded so small and pitiful Abby wanted to cry.

"Sure, you can." Abby pushed off the couch and went into the kitchen, adrenaline still pumping from the scare. "Stupid board. Stupid old house. Stupid, stupid, stupid."

As she railed against the accident, she opened the cabinet for a glass, and another chip of paint fell from the overpainted wood.

She needed a new house. A place that wasn't a danger to Lila.

Abby leaned her forehead against the cabinet and fought off the surge of pride. Brady Buchanon's voice played in her memory. He could give Lila something she needed.

As hard as it would be for Abby to accept charity again, this wasn't about her. This was about doing the right thing for Lila.

She dug in her pocket and pulled out the card with the blue Buchanon Built logo and Brady's number, and resigned herself to a little more humiliation.

Chapter Three

"You have to be kidding me?" Grimly, Brady leaned a shoulder against one unfinished wall of gypsum board, his cell phone pressed against his ear. He gripped the device as if he wanted to strangle someone. Which he did. "When did this happen?"

He listened as his father railed against yet another act of vandalism against one of the company's building sites. No one could figure out why Buchanon Built was being targeted, but someone seemed to know when a home-in-progress would be devoid of workers.

"I'll sleep here if I have to, but this project is not going to be damaged." Brady shuddered at the thought. They'd chunked thousands into this showplace along Crystal Ridge. A break-in could set them back for months and cost them more than the insurance could cover.

His father ranted, growing louder by the minute, as if the situation was entirely Brady's fault.

"Right. I hear you, Dad. Call Leroy at the police station. He knows about the others."

When he tapped the End key a few minutes later, his blood boiled and his finger trembled. What a lousy day. The trenchers had hit an electric cable and downed all the power in the Huckleberry Creek addition. A frame carpenter had been taken to the ER with appendicitis. Dad was furious over the lack of a plumber on the Edwards house. And now this. Another Buchanon Built home damaged by thugs.

He ran a hand over the top of his head and debated on a trip to the damaged site or staying with this project for the remainder of the day. Not much he could do over there until the police had made another useless investigation. Dad was already there and mad enough to spit nails faster and harder than an air gun.

Here was preferable at the moment.

From the back room, a table saw revved up in a high-pitched wail. The twins were on it, trimming out the bedrooms in a unique routered design created specifically for this house by the Buchanon brain trust.

His phone vibrated again. Brady groaned. Loudly. *Please. Not more trouble.*

"Hello," he growled into the mouthpiece, daring the caller to give him one more bit of bad news.

No one said anything for a couple of seconds, and then a very hesitant female voice asked, "Is this Brady Buchanon?"

A pleasant voice, sweet and warm and womanly.

Nice. But who?

His brain played mental gymnastics as he softened his reply, "Yes, this is Brady. May I ask who's calling?"

"Abby Webster. Have I caught you at a bad time?"

He almost laughed. She didn't know the half of it. "Not at all. What can I do for you, Abby? Maybe a little remodel work?"

He couldn't help it. He was born to be pushy when he wanted something. She'd probably turn him down again, but he had to try.

"Actually—" there was that hesitation again "—yes."

The word hummed through the cyberspace connecting them. She'd said yes?

"You changed your mind? May I ask why?" A smile lit his insides, erasing some of the lousy, lousy events of the day. Teasing, he said, "Was it my charm, or my pretty brothers? Or maybe the double order of French toast?"

He didn't—wouldn't—mention the tip.

She sighed out a weary breath. "Blame it on my front porch. I fell through."

Brady's shoulders tensed. "Are you hurt?"

"No, but I had Lila in my arms. She wasn't hurt either, but she could have been." Her words faded in an anguished breath.

Brady got her meaning. She didn't particularly want the makeover, but for Lila she'd take it. He didn't care what her reasons were. In the end, she'd be delighted with the results, and Lila would be better off while he got to play Santa. A win-win in his book any day of the week.

Already feeling vastly better, he said, "Let's get together tonight and talk this over. I'll come by after work."

"Well, I—guess that would be okay."

"Do you and Lila like barbecue?"

"What? Yes, we love it, but you don't need to bring food."

Brady laughed. "Abby, I'm a big boy. I gotta have food, and so do you." Even though he couldn't recall a time when he'd brought food for a prospective client. That was his sister's domain. "What time works best?"

After a few more useless protests against him doing anything nice for her, she named the time and they ended the call.

His mood much elevated, he slid his cell phone into his back pocket and gave a soft whistle. "Quitting time, Dawg."

The canine, sprawled in a corner of the great room

like an ornament befitting the massive fireplace, lifted his brindled body from the bare concrete floor and gave his fur a hardy shake.

"We're going to Abby Webster's, and I might let you say hello. What do ya think about that?"

Dawg trotted to the door and looked back expectantly.

The dog was weird that way. He seemed to know what Brady was talking about most of the time. "Hold on a minute. I have to tell the other guys."

Feeling unusually chipper, considering the problems of the day, Brady cleaned up his mess and secured his tools before talking to the twins.

"Another break-in," he said as he entered what would be the master bedroom. At the moment, sawdust covered the floor, along with a stack of clean-smelling lumber. Smack in the middle of the room stood a table saw and one of his brothers in plastic safety goggles. "Dad called."

Sawyer pushed the goggles atop his black hair and tilted his chin toward the unfinished ceiling in a pained groan. "That must have been fun."

"Loved it," Brady answered wryly. "You boys about ready to call it a night?" He rubbed his hands together. "I've got places to go and things to do."

Dawson, on his haunches fitting trim, pushed to a stand. "You seem in a seriously good mood for someone who's been talking to Dad about vandalism. Don't tell me you have a date."

"Nah, nothing like that." Although he was taking food and going to see a woman, the reason had nothing to do with a date. It was all about the project, not the woman. "Dad's not the only caller. Get this. Abby Webster changed her mind. The makeover is on!" He pumped a fist.

A grin deepened the single dimple in Dawson's cheek. "Yeah? That's terrific. When do we start?"

"I'm headed over there later tonight to work out plans. This should be the best makeover ever."

The twins exchanged looks.

Brady pointed two index fingers, one at each brother. "Don't start that. Abby's not the only single-mom make-over we've done."

Dawson held up both palms. "Hey, I'm with you. I was over there, remember. Nobody in town needs this remodel more than Abby and her little girl."

"Yeah, the little girl," Brady said. "She's the kicker."

Sawyer spiked an eyebrow in his usual tease. "And the mom's no slouch."

No, Brady thought, surprising himself. No, she wasn't.

Abby's nerves jittered as she opened the door for Brady Buchanon. He came inside, bringing with him the scent of hot, spicy barbecue.

"I can tell what's in that sack," she said as he handed it over. "The smell is fabulous."

"Danny makes the best barbecue in this part of Texas."

She knew, though budget constraints had meant she hadn't eaten any of it in a long time. Eating out was a luxury reserved for Lila's clinic visits when they really had no choice.

"You didn't have to bring dinner."

Brady shrugged. "It's just food."

Lila, who was lying on her belly on the rug sorting through a bag of magnetic shapes, held one up.

"This is a wetangle," she said.

"Rectangle," Abby corrected, unsure if Brady would understand Lila's developing speech.

"I see that." The big man went to his haunches beside her daughter. "Do you know any of the others?"

"Yes." And she named off the circle, square and heart, making her mama proud.

"I brought you something." From inside his jacket he took a small, stuffed animal. "I hope you like dogs."

"A puppy!" Lila's eyes lit up as Abby's suddenly filled with unexpected tears. "Mama, look. A puppy. I love him."

Abby wanted to protest the unnecessary gift, but how could she when it had made Lila so happy?

"Brady," she simply said, shaking her head. Why had he done that? They weren't friends or relatives. They barely knew each other.

Brady ignored her protest. He was, she noticed again, good at that.

"I have a dog outside in my truck," he said to her beaming daughter. "Want to see him?"

Lila's eyes grew wide. "A real one?"

"As real as can be."

"What's his name?"

"Dawg."

With an odd hitch beneath her ribs, Abby listened to the easy conversation between her child and the giant man. Lila, accustomed to doctors and technicians and physical therapists, rarely met a stranger, but it was the man who bothered Abby. He couldn't be for real. She knew that for a fact. People were nice in the beginning but after a while, they'd disappoint you.

Someday Lila would learn those things the hard way, a truth that made Abby ache. But today Lila was an innocent, trusting child clearly fascinated by the idea of a real dog, something she'd never had.

"Does he like little girls?" Lila asked.

"Crazy for them."

"Will he jump on me?"

"Not if I tell him to be good."

"I want to pet him." In total trust, Lila reached her arms up toward Brady. "Let's go."

"Do you mind?" he said, rather belatedly to Abby.

Abby scoffed softly. Even if she minded, he'd put her in an impossible situation. "You don't have to do that."

"I want to."

She wanted to ask why he'd bother when he'd come to discuss the remodel, but instead she said, "Go ahead. She loves animals, especially dogs."

Those mesmerizing blue eyes sparkled. "I gathered that by her reaction to the stuffed one." To Lila, he said, "Come on, little one. Up you go."

He dwarfed her child, this huge man with the handsome face and stunning eyes, but he was as gentle as a whisper as he lifted Lila into his arms.

A big, big man. Her tiny, precious girl.

Something tender moved inside Abby.

She whipped away to open the door, but Brady with his long stride beat her there and easily maneuvered both the door and the child.

"Watch that board," she warned, suddenly scared that his superior size would send him plummeting with Lila as she had done.

"Got it." He stepped over the opening.

Abby walked alongside, aware of Brady Buchanon in the most uncomfortable way. His kindness bewildered her. Not once since his arrival had he mentioned the makeover. Or the fact that she was the Buchanon charity case for the year.

The twenty-dollar bill was in her back pocket. She should return it, remind him that she didn't want his pity or his charity and that she was only accepting the makeover for Lila's sake. Even that stuck in her craw like a dry slice of toast. *She* wanted to provide for her daughter.

As they approached the blue pickup, a large brindle-colored dog with soulful golden eyes and a sweet expression stuck his head out the open driver's-side window.

"He thinks he can drive," Brady said, eliciting a giggle from Lila. "You can pet him. He's a big sap. He'll love it."

Lila placed a tentative hand on the dog's wide head. When he didn't move, only looked at her with those sweet eyes, she ruffled his ears. "Can he come out and play?"

"Sure. Open the door for him, will you, Abby?" He said the words casually, and she could see he felt comfortable with people in a way she didn't. But then, the Buchanons were a large family.

She opened the truck door, and the dog named Dawg leaped gracefully to the ground and stared up at his owner as if waiting for commands.

"Sit down, Dawg. This is Lila and Abby. Friends. Be good now."

The dog flopped on his rear, long tail bumping the ground with comical eagerness. Brady went down on the balls of his feet in front of the animal with Lila on one khaki-clad knee. Abby watched as Dawg behaved like a gentleman while Lila petted him.

"He likes me," Lila said.

"He sure does. Hold your hand out like this." Brady took Lila's tiny hand and turned it palm up. "Now say, 'Dawg, shake.'"

Lila did as Brady asked. When Dawg carefully plopped a furry paw into her palm, her giggle sent happy chills down Abby's spine.

"He did it! Mommy, Dawg shaked my hand."

"Is he always this well behaved?" Abby asked.

"Pretty much. I take him on the job with me." Brady hitched a shoulder. "Basically take him everywhere. He has to behave or be stuck at home alone."

"Do you let him inside the house?"

"Sure. He sleeps at the end of my bed."

Okay, that was too much information. She didn't want

to imagine a sleep-rumpled Brady in baggy pajama pants. He was a builder, here to do a job.

"Mama, can he come inside? Dawg can sit by me. I'll show him my shapes."

Abby hesitated. To Brady, she said, "Should I let him?"

"Up to you, but he won't be a problem. I can promise you that."

Promises. She knew how those worked.

"I suppose it's all right this once. What kind of dog is he?"

"Anyone's guess. Some boxer, shepherd, Lab. Who knows? I got him from the shelter, but we don't care, do we, pal? We're all mutts in our way." With one final pat on the dog's head, Brady rose with Lila. The dog trotted along behind as they returned to the house.

Abby was keenly aware of the man who gently put her daughter on the floor mat, commanded the dog to behave and followed Abby into the kitchen.

Uncomfortable and uncertain, she asked, "Do you want to talk while we eat? Or after?"

This was not a social call. He'd surely want to do his business and move on. The Buchanons were busy people, involved in many segments of Gabriel's Crossing life.

"Might as well eat while the barbecue and fries are hot. Talk can happen anytime."

Though her kitchen-dining space was minuscule and made smaller by the invasion of a man the size of some mythological warrior, Brady made himself at home. He opened cabinets, found plates and knives, and generally embarrassed her.

"I can do this," she said, grabbing the utensils from him.

"Many hands make light work." He grinned. "That's according to my Grandfather Buchanon who started the construction company. Having a bunch of grandsons made work easier for him."

She quickly set out the dishes and food, going a little mushy to discover a foam container of macaroni in the bag.

He'd remembered Lila's love of all things macaroni?

Who was this guy?

"I'll get the little one," he said, and ducked his head beneath the doorway as he went into the living room.

During their meal, Brady talked about everything but the makeover. He drew her out, asking questions about her work, Lila's school, Christmas and all things Gabriel's Crossing. He told her a funny story about his sisters and a skunk, and Abby found herself relating funny experiences from the café. Then they shared a laugh about the ongoing feud between Hoss Hanover, town mayor, and Flo Dubois, a former Vegas showgirl now in her seventies and still as sassy and ornery as ever.

Once or twice, she even forgot he was here on a charitable mission.

By the time the messy barbecue was demolished, the nervous butterflies in her stomach had subsided. Brady might be big but he wasn't nearly as scary as she'd thought.

"Well," he said, pushing his plate aside. "That was good. Now my brain can work. Let's talk makeover."

She held up a finger. "First, you have to know something. I'm only doing this because of Lila."

He aimed those swimming-pool eyes at her. "Understood. Now, let's get down to basics. I'll do a walk-through and make notes of what needs done. Then, we'll talk about it. I want your input, your ideas, what you want and need. I have people on my team who know all about special-needs construction. They'll be in on the planning, too, but basically this project is my baby. Mine and yours."

She was feeling a little overwhelmed. "I don't even know what to say."

"No need to say anything. I'll bring by appliance catalogs, color charts, carpet samples and that kind of thing for you to look at." He flashed a smile. "That's where you come in."

Carpet? Appliances? "I didn't expect all that."

In truth, she hadn't expected anything, but this…this. She was starting to get excited. Not good. Not good at all. Excitement preceded disappointment.

As usual, Brady paid her no mind. He took a notepad from his jacket hanging on the back of a chair. "If it's all right, I'll inspect the structure first, get a basic idea of what we'll need to do, and we'll go from there."

"Sure. I'll just… Can I follow you around?"

He chuckled. "It's your house."

Leaving Lila to watch a *Veggie Tales* with Dawg sprawled adoringly at her side, Abby joined the builder. As they did the walk-through, she saw the house in a new light, from a stranger's viewpoint, and shame trickled into her stomach.

He must think she was a sorry excuse for a mother, raising her special-needs daughter in a run-down house with nothing more than a safety bar beside the bathtub.

"I installed that myself," she said, half in self-defense. She didn't want him judging her. She tried. And for now, she could carry Lila. "I was planning to add more as she grows."

"You did great." But he jotted all kinds of notes on that pad of his as he inspected plumbing under the sinks and thumped his big fist against walls. She cringed at the last, concerned he'd go right through.

"We could create a bathroom here specifically for her. Put a walk-in shower there," he said. "Big enough to accommodate her walker or a wheelchair. Add some bench seating, lower the sink and commode so she can access them herself."

The ideas made Abby's heart soar and her eyes water. "That would be wonderful. I don't know how to thank you."

"No thanks needed. Gotta make things right for the little princess." He winked. "Dawg said so."

She smiled, grateful to him for making light of a humiliating situation. For her, anyway.

They moved through the house and her brain spun as he discussed removing walls, widening halls and rearranging the interior of the house for more space and flow.

Hope, that sneaky weed, sprouted up inside her chest. His ideas were wonderful, beautiful, a dream come true. He was amazing, kind and funny, and Abby found herself looking forward to the days and hours he'd spend in her house making it better.

Though the decision had come slowly, like Cinderella preparing for the ball, she now wanted this makeover badly. For Lila's sake. Brady really could give her child what she needed.

When they entered her bedroom, Abby was thankful she'd made the bed and tidied up before his arrival. She lingered in the doorway, a little disconcerted to have him in her private space. But she'd have to get used to that, she supposed. He was a builder; he didn't think anything about it.

Brady pointed to the ceiling and exterior wall. "Some leakage in here."

"Only when it rains." She tried to sound chipper, but Brady frowned and her stomach dipped. "Will that be a problem?"

"Depends." He walked across to the window and the wooden floor groaned. He paused, bounced a little and frowned again. "Where's your crawl space? Lots of weak spots in the flooring. I'd better have a look at the joists before we get too far into this."

She didn't know a joist from a joust, but she knew where the crawl space was, though she couldn't imagine a man his size crawling under her house. "You'll get dirty."

Humor brightened his face. "I'm in construction. We get a little dirty."

"Yes, but you're the owner."

"A hands-on owner. Dad insisted we know the business from the ground up. Literally." He rotated his wide shoulders and looked down at his large body. "Though nowadays I usually send someone smaller under the houses."

"I fixed a broken pipe last winter. I could go under there and tell you what I see."

"Don't worry. I got it. Be right back."

"You'll need a flashlight."

"In my truck."

He headed outside while she checked on Lila and Dawg, and then started on kitchen cleanup. She heard him clang on a pipe with something metal, so she knew he'd somehow squeezed into the small space.

He was gone for quite a while and when he came inside, he didn't look happy.

Putting away the last dish, she dried her hands, worry niggling.

"You have spiderwebs—"

His chin dipped toward his shoulder. "Where?"

"Your hair. Bend down." Without thinking anything of it, she dusted the cobwebs from his russet hair and the back of his shirt. The action felt intimate somehow, and she finished quickly.

"Sorry. I thought I knocked them off outside."

A little dust on the floor was the least of her concerns. "What's the verdict?"

"Not what I'd hoped. Or expected."

"What does that mean?"

"Sit down. Let's talk a minute." He motioned to the table.

They'd been talking for two hours, but she pulled out a chair and sat. He did the same. A knot formed in her belly. Something was wrong.

"I have bad news, Abby." Brady pinched the top of his lip, drew in a deep breath and blew it out in a hearty gust. "Your house is not salvageable. I can't do the remodel."

Chapter Four

Abby had known it was too good to be true. She shouldn't be disappointed. But she was. Which was exactly what she got for getting her hopes up. She knew better.

"Is it that bad?" Sure, the old house leaked and was draftier than a barn, but she and Lila lived in reasonable comfort. Except when it rained. Or the north wind blew.

"Bad enough that it isn't cost-effective to remodel."

"Okay." She nodded once. She'd been let down before. At least she hadn't started dreaming and planning too much. Maybe a little when he'd mentioned color charts and carpet samples.

She put on her best fake smile and stood. "Thank you for trying. I appreciate the thought and your time, and I'm sure you'll have no problem finding someone else for your Christmas makeover. It's a wonderful thing you do."

Brady titled his head and lifted his index finger. "Whoa, wait a second. I didn't say I was giving up. Buchanons never give up."

"But if you can't repair the problems—"

"There's always a way." He twitched a shoulder. "We can start fresh, build new."

"What?" She slithered back onto the chair, more than a little stunned. Was he serious? Build new?

"Makeovers come in many forms. Remodel. Brand-new. In your situation, we'll shoot for new. We can bulldoze this house and build exactly what you want in its place."

Abby refused to acknowledge the sudden, thrilling anticipation frolicking in her belly. What he asked was impossible. Completely impossible. Even though the property was hers to do with as she pleased, she had no place else to go. Bulldozing to build new was out of the question! "I don't think so, Brady."

"Why not? I can build bigger, better and more efficient from the ground up, a house exactly the way you want it. With all the bells and whistles and lots of pretty things for Lila."

Oh, he was cruel, dangling that carrot in front of her. For a fleeting moment the image of a perfect little cottage with fresh paint and matching shutters surrounded by colorful flowers flashed through her mind. A dream home for her and Lila. A place that would assist Lila to develop her strengths rather than inhibit her.

Then reality, that cruel beast, came roaring back. Some things just weren't possible. "Thank you, but it won't work."

"Sure it will," he said with the confidence only a successful man with an easy upbringing would display. "Starting fresh is the perfect solution."

He clearly hadn't been kicked in the teeth very many times, and he had no understanding of a person without alternatives, with no place to go, no one but herself to lean on. "This place may not look like much to you, Brady, but this is our home. There's nothing perfect about tearing it down. We live here."

"You can live somewhere else temporarily. It won't be long. My crews work fast."

She wanted to accept his offer so badly her throat ached from holding back a shout of *Yes!*

"I can't," she said instead. "Please understand, as much

as I appreciate the offer, I like my home the way it is." And frogs had wings. "Lila and I are fine right here."

She wasn't about to admit that she had nowhere else to go, no money for another monthly payment on a rental and no relatives to impose upon.

He tilted back in his chair and pinched his upper lip. He had a habit of doing that, she noticed, when things weren't going his way. He breathed in through his nose and out through his mouth in a puff of frustration. His blue eyes, laser bright, dimmed the slightest amount.

"You're saying no?" He seemed incredulous as if only an idiot would turn down a brand-new house, and she wasn't going to explain the circumstances to change his assessment. It was bad enough he pitied her living conditions; she sure didn't want him to know the rest.

"Yes." From the living room, she heard Lila giggle and fought off a surge of longing. Her baby deserved better.

She stood again and this time Brady stood with her, towering over her. There was something comforting about a nice man who could make her feel small and feminine.

Teeth clamped tight against the bizarre emotions Brady Buchanon elicited, she led the way into the living room.

Dawg was lying with his nose on Lila's lap. Her tiny hand rested on his wide head as they both watched cartoons. The dog lifted his eyes toward his master. Brady nudged his chin toward the door. "Time to go, boy."

Slowly, Dawg stretched to his feet.

"Oh," Lila said, and wrapped her arms around the animal's neck.

"Brady and Dawg have to leave now, Lila. Tell them bye."

Lila looked as if her best friend forever was abandoning her. She gave Dawg one final squeeze. "Bye, Dawg. Bye, Mr. Brady."

Brady, whose jaw was tight, as if he held back a hearty

temper, softened. He gave one of Lila's twin ponytails a gentle tug. "Bye now, little one."

Stiffly Abby opened the front door, eager now for him to leave so she could forget this had happened, forget she'd almost let herself dream. "Thank you for the barbecue."

She didn't know if she was making the right choice or not, but for her, refusal was the only choice.

"So how's the home makeover going?" Dawson asked as he plopped down next to Brady on the couch at Mom's house the next Sunday afternoon.

"It's not." Brady stuck his hand in the chip bowl and filled his paw with Fritos and tossed one to Dawg.

"No?" Sawyer joined the pair in the family room waiting for the NFL game to come on. From the kitchen came smells of hot Ro*Tel cheese dip and homemade chili as the seven siblings gathered for the weekly after-church hangout and football frenzy. "Why not?"

"Abby changed her mind." Brady was, he had to admit, pretty steamed about that little turn of events. What kind of woman turned down a new house when she could obviously use it, especially when her kid had needs that weren't being addressed by her current residence? And the way she'd refused, without so much as a reason, irritated him.

"I thought she was on board." Dawson crunched down on a chip. "What did you do?"

"You think this is my fault?" Like the fiasco on the Crystal Ridge building site. According to Dad, Brady should have foreseen the decorative-rock mix-up. Now he had an entire fireplace to demolish and start all over, as if deadlines weren't tight enough. Even the church service, where he usually found some peace, hadn't eased the stress tightening the back of his shoulders. This deal with Abby was the straw that broke the camel's back.

He glared at his twin brothers—first Sawyer and then

Dawson had blamed him for the problem. If steam wasn't coming out of his ears, he'd be surprised. He'd enjoyed that barbecue supper with Abby Webster and her little girl. Maybe that's what bugged him most. He'd liked her. He thought she liked him.

Dawson raised both hands in surrender. "You'll hear no blame from me. I only meant, what's going on? Why did she back out?"

"Who knows? Abby Webster is the strangest, most stubborn woman I've ever encountered."

Dawson gave him a long look. "I thought you liked her."

"Yeah, well, the feeling wasn't mutual, I guess. She showed me the door."

"So, what did she say?"

"Just that she couldn't. It wouldn't work."

"Couldn't what? What wouldn't work?" Sawyer, the mirror twin to Dawson, stretched his long legs out on the floor next to the sofa. By the time the game started there would be Buchanons all over the room. Brady was happy he'd gotten here first to grab a seat on the couch, but he usually ended up on the floor with Dawg.

He had a quick flash of Dawg on the floor of Abby's house with Lila, the angel-drawing charmer. He'd seen her pink ankle braces and the walker she used for balance. Abby's house, with the crooked floors and raised thresholds, was a hazard to Lila. He really wanted to do that makeover for the little girl.

"Long story short, the house is a wreck. Joist rotted, leaks everywhere, bad plumbing. There's so much wrong, I wouldn't spend a dime to remodel it."

"Then you're the one who backed out," Dawson said. "I knew I should have gone with you."

"No." Brady frowned at a Frito and then at his brother. "I offered a new house instead of the remodel. Raze the old one, build from the ground up. It's only a matter of time until she'll have no choice but to move." He'd never built from ground up before on one of his makeovers, but why not?

Dawson turned a bewildered face in his direction. "She turned down a new house?"

"Flat. No reason. Just no."

"That *is* weird."

"See?" He pointed a Frito. "I told you."

"Her little girl sure is cute. Kind of gets you right here." Dawson tapped his chest with a fist. "I thought Abby would go for it for her sake."

"Yeah." Brady popped the chip in his mouth and considered going to the kitchen for the Ro*Tel dip. "Pretty adorable kid."

"A kid who needs a handicap-accessible house."

"I don't get it," Sawyer said. He dragged a throw pillow from the sofa and shoved it under his dark head. "Why would the mom refuse? Makes no sense."

"Take it from the top, Brady," Dawson said. "What exactly went down? She was on board before you mentioned the rebuild. When did things go sour?"

Brady related the conversation, trying his best to remember the exact point when Abby backed away. "It was the demolition. She said it would never work. After that—" He drew a finger across his throat. "The project was dead."

"Hmm." Dawson pushed back against the cushions of Mom's enormous gray sectional. His Dallas Cowboys jersey stretched across his lean, toned chest. Like all the Buchanon brothers, he'd played college football and was still a fanatic about the game. "She said it wouldn't work? Wonder what she meant by that? What wouldn't work?"

Brady's shoulders hitched. "You got me. I promised a fast rebuild so she wouldn't have to live elsewhere very long."

Dawson snapped his fingers and leaned forward. "Could that be the problem?"

"What? She didn't believe we could work that fast?"

"No. The living-elsewhere part."

"I don't know what you mean."

"I get it." Sawyer sat up and thumped the pillow with his fist. "Maybe she doesn't have another place to live. Or maybe money for the rent, even for a few months, would be prohibitive. A waitress doesn't make much money, and with the little girl's special needs…"

"True, but they could stay with relatives," Dawson said.

Brady shook his head. "According to my sources, she doesn't have any. Grew up in foster care, I think, and her little girl's father skipped out on her before Lila was born. It's just Abby and Lila against the world, which was part of the reason I chose them."

"That poor girl." Karen Buchanon breezed into the room bearing hot cheese dip. Behind her was Brady's adored younger sister, Allison, a peanut of a woman with dark, flippy hair. Her fiancé, Jake Hamilton, once an outcast in the Buchanon household, would show up at some point in the afternoon after checking on his cattle and his grandmother.

"I never considered her living arrangements, but that could be the problem," Brady admitted. "Maybe she has nowhere to go."

"And no spare money for a rental, even a cheap one." Dawson took both hands, rotated his head and popped his neck. "Crick," he said to no one in particular.

Brady arched an eyebrow. "You don't get much cheaper than her house."

"But it's hers."

"I wonder why she didn't simply tell me she had no place else to live during the rebuild. If that's the case."

"Oh, Brady." His mother stood behind Dawson and began kneading his shoulders. "If the girl has any pride at all, which she clearly does, she wouldn't tell you such a thing. No one wants to be pitied."

Brady opened his mouth and then closed it again, the salty taste of chips making him thirsty. "You think that's her problem?"

"Makes sense to me," Dawson said, settling into his mother's massage with his eyes closed. "Though it's your problem, not hers."

"Ditto," said Sawyer.

Brady had always been surrounded by a huge family, sometimes to the point of smothering. He couldn't fathom anyone being completely alone, but if Abby Webster had no one but her four-year-old daughter, she was a pretty amazing woman. Really amazing. She'd bought a house, such as it was, and balanced a job with the needs of her special child. Lila was clearly loved and well cared for.

"I guess I embarrassed her."

"No doubt about it." His mom left Dawson's side to pat Brady's shoulder. "But you meant well, honey."

Brady put his big paw over her hand. "Thanks, Mom. Any ideas of how to fix it?"

"Fix it? No. But I might have an idea of how to get her out of that house so you can build her a new one. Dad won't mind."

"If it involves Dad, forget it. He's against the project this year."

"I heard." She smiled. "But you're going to do it anyway, aren't you?"

"If I can convince Abby to let me."

"Good." She tugged at her pressed slacks and perched on the arm of an easy chair. "Abby's excited about the makeover. She wants it, son."

"How do you know this?"

"Jan, Abby's boss, talked to me at the BPW meeting." Mom was president of the local chapter of Business and Professional Women. "She was thrilled for Abby. She also told me what a hard worker Abby is and how well she takes care of her little girl. According to Jan, no one deserves your makeover any more than Abby and Lila Webster. That's why I'm willing to step in and help out."

Brady looked at his mother in awe. "Is there anything in this town you don't know?"

Her eyes crinkled. "Not much."

Sawyer snorted. Dawson just smiled. Allison found an empty space next to Sawyer, curled her little feet beneath her and reached for the dip.

"Yeah, well, that still doesn't solve the problem. I can't move her in with me." Though the thought didn't exactly repulse him. Dawg would be thrilled.

"But *I* can move her in with *me*."

Four sets of sibling eyes turned to their mother. She pushed back a lock of tidy blond hair, a cat's smile on her lips.

"Since you kids built your own places, Dad and I ramble around in this big old, empty house. We've got the room. Abby needs a temporary place to stay, and a child always makes Christmas season more fun. So why not?"

"You'd do that?" Brady didn't know why he was asking. Of course, she'd do it. In the past, she'd mothered a number of foreign-exchange students along with her brood of seven. And that didn't count the handfuls of friends and relatives who'd lived temporarily in the Buchanon house, including Jake, Allison's fiancé. Mom loved having the house filled with people.

"I think it's a great idea." This from Allison.

Brady, for all the hope suddenly surging through his veins, had his doubts. Mom might be on board, but what would Abby think? The Buchanons were strangers to her, and the family didn't know Abby like he knew Abby. She was stubborn, prideful, independent to a fault. Pretty, too, he'd noticed, though why his thoughts had gone in that direction he couldn't fathom. "I don't know. Think she'll go for it?"

Mom arched one eyebrow and reached for a chip. "There's only one way to find out."

"Someone here to see you, Abby. Take a break."

Abby slid a tray of dishes onto the sink in the back of the diner and turned toward her boss. The noon rush had passed but there was still plenty to do. "Who is it?"

"Karen Buchanon."

"*Karen* Buchanon?" If Jan had said Brady, she wouldn't have been surprised. In fact, she'd probably have gotten that jittery wiggle in her stomach, a totally stupid reaction to a man she barely knew. But he was a good guy who could cause Prince Charming fantasies even in a hard nut like her. She also felt a little guilty for upsetting him. He'd offered an act of kindness and she'd shot him down.

Yesterday, he'd come into the Buttered Biscuit with a big grin and a crazy invitation for her and Lila to temporarily move in with his parents while he built her brand-new house. Even though her heart had leaped at the offer, he could not have been serious. Well intentioned, yes. Serious, no way.

She didn't know the Buchanons. They didn't know her. Things like that didn't happen except in movies. And how had he known a decent place to live was her primary reason for rejecting the makeover?

Five minutes later, as she sat across an open table from the blonde and lovely Buchanon matriarch, she learned how serious Brady had been. "Mrs. Buchanon, please don't take this the wrong way, but why? Why would you open your home to a complete stranger?"

"My family has been tremendously blessed, and we believe that caring about others is not only a directive from the Lord but it makes us happier people. We love to give. Brady's gifts are in his ability to build, and he loves giving away a Buchanon Built home at Christmas. He plans for it and looks forward to it all year."

Abby fidgeted with the saltshaker, realized what she was doing and shoved it back to the side of the table. Brady had hinted that the Buchanons were devout Christians, but so were lots of people in Texas and none of them gave away houses. At least none that she knew about. "There are other people in Gabriel's Crossing who could use a makeover."

"My son's heart is the biggest part of him and, as I'm sure you've noticed, that's saying a lot. When Brady sets his sights on something, he's a bulldog."

"But why me?"

"It's the way Brady's made. He picked you and you're it." She folded her hands atop the table. "I do know this. He was taken with your little girl. He told the family about her, showed us the angel she drew him and even hung it on his refrigerator."

A piece of pride chipped away. "He did?"

Karen nodded. "'An angel from an angel,' he said. Now, we're all anxious to meet her. She must be amazing."

"Oh, she is. Lila is the kindest, funniest, smartest, most resilient—" She caught herself and laughed, self-conscious and sure her warm face glowed pink. "Sorry. I get a little carried away about my daughter. She's everything to me."

"Then do this for her, Abby. Let Brady build your house. Give that amazing daughter of yours a new home for Christmas. And give us the pleasure of knowing your special little girl."

Unbidden tears welled in Abby's eyes. Buchanons didn't play fair.

Karen leaned forward. "I respect your pride. I even admire it, but say yes for your daughter's sake. We'll make the transition as easy as possible. My girls and I will help you pack, and the boys can have you moved in a single day. There's plenty of storage at the company warehouse for your extra things."

Abby wasn't about to admit she didn't have much extra

sitting around. Her pride was aching as it was, and her cynical inner voice was screaming in her ear. No one does something for nothing. If she went along with this, she had to remember that.

"You really are serious?"

"Absolutely. You'd be doing us a favor." Karen waved a hand and a diamond flashed, another reminder of the chasm between Abby Webster and the Buchanons. "Our house is too big with the kids gone. Imagine, a house that has raised seven kids and welcomed an endless array of their friends. A house of noise and activity and energy. Now, the place is too quiet all the time. Frankly, it's lonely without the laughter of children."

"Lila is special-needs."

"No worries about that. We added accessibility when Dan's father moved in with us after his stroke. She can move around most of the house without a problem. We'll make sure Lila has whatever she needs."

"I meant she's not like other children and never will be. Potty training is still ongoing. She uses a walker and braces but still crawls at times. We have therapy exercises every night and activities to encourage independence. Living with a spina bifida child can be a challenge, and some people are put off by her differences."

Karen sat back, her serene brown eyes locked on Abby's. "Honey, God made us all with special needs. Some are simply more apparent than others. Lila will find welcome at my house. More than welcome. I promise you."

Buchanons were good at tossing out promises. She couldn't help wonder if they'd keep them.

Abby pulled the napkin holder toward her and straightened the narrow sheets in the dispenser. The back side needed a refill.

A few afternoon coffee drinkers sat at the counter talking politics, and at a side table near the window where he could keep a watchful eye, police deputy Leroy was having his pie break. Apple à la mode. The smell of cinnamon reminded her of the coming holidays. Jan would want them to decorate the café soon.

Wouldn't it be wonderful to have a beautiful new home to decorate?

She was fidgeting, scared to say yes and knowing she'd be a fool to turn down the best offer she'd ever had. How many people had a chance like this to give their child a custom-built, handicap-accessible home, free of added payments? Certainly not someone like her, who could barely stretch her paycheck to the end of each month.

"This is kind of overwhelming," she admitted.

"If it would make you feel better, come to the house for dinner tonight, get acquainted, see the house and then decide. You and Lila will have your own private space. We won't crowd you."

"I'd expect to help with the chores." The gesture was pure self-preservation.

"And I'd take you up on that." Karen's mouth curved. "What time do you get off work?"

"Six."

"Dinner at seven, then? Is that too early?"

"No. Seven is perfect."

"Here's the address." Karen scribbled on the back of a Buchanon Built business card and pushed it across the table.

Abby knew where they lived. Gabriel's Crossing wasn't that big. She stared at the address and wrung her hands. "Are you sure about this?"

Karen laughed as she picked up her handbag and scooted back her chair. "Abby, you fret too much. See you at seven."

Chapter Five

Abby and Lila moved in the next Saturday. Or rather, three Buchanon males, minus the older brother, Quinn, along with Jake Hamilton, all in pickup trucks, roared into her front yard at eight o'clock to do the heavy lifting.

She'd worked frantically all week, staying up late each night after work to pack her belongings into boxes. When Karen had called to set a date for packing, she was surprised that Abby was finished. A girl had to keep control of something!

The truth was, she was letting herself get too excited about the project, and Lila was over the moon. The night they'd gone to dinner at the Buchanon house, she'd suffered a longing so deep, she'd lain awake later wondering what it would have been like to have grown up in that house with Karen and Dan Buchanon. Wondering what it would be like for Lila to have grandparents like them to dote on her.

Brady had come for dinner, too, and turned her mushy by the sweet way he interacted with her little girl. Though Dan Buchanon wasn't as effusive as his wife and son, he'd been kind to Lila, who could charm the quills off a porcupine.

"Let the games begin." Brady, looking too good for words, leaped from his truck cab with Dawg right behind and rubbed his hands together with glee. The rest of the men piled out of their vehicles and started tossing around furniture like dollhouse toys.

Abby had a moment of misgiving. She was developing a killer crush on Brady Buchanon, a feeling she would have to keep under wraps. The Websters from the wrong side of the tracks were not in the same league with the prominent, successful Buchanons. She and Lila were a project, a charity case. She needed to keep that front and center in her thinking. A crush was normal. Anything more was off-limits.

As it was, Brady slapped her a high five as he entered the house and headed straight for Lila, whose big brown eyes were wider than saucers. Abby understood. She was feeling a little overwhelmed herself.

"There she is," he exclaimed. "Princess Lila." He scooped the little one up into his big arms. "Look here, boys. Meet Lila. She's the best angel drawer this side of the Red River."

Lila's face glowed with the attention. "Did you bring Dawg?"

"Sure, I did. He's outside, though. Didn't want him underfoot while we work. Want to hang out with him?"

Abby came alongside the pair as the Buchanon twins ducked into Lila's bedroom to begin the move. The jitters started up again. This was really happening. "I'll take her outside to play, so she won't be in the way."

Brady didn't relinquish his hold on Lila. "You could take her over to the folks' if you want to. We'll be back and forth."

"No." She shook her head. There was something wonderful about being here, watching them work with the knowledge of what was to come. "I'd rather stay if it's okay. I'll keep Lila out of the way."

"Sure. No problem. Whatever you want. Just don't want her to get bumped or stepped on." His cell phone chirped.

She took Lila from his arms so he could answer. Jake, the cowboy who'd won Allison Buchanon's heart, drifted by with a stack of boxes marked "kitchen." The twins, Dawson and Sawyer, shuffled past with Lila's dresser.

"Hey, Dad. What's up?" Brady turned slightly and Abby stepped back to give him some privacy. "Yes. I told you about the substitution on the Jefferson house, remember? It can't be helped. The supplier is out of that particular color."

The voice on the other end grew loud enough that Abby could tell he wasn't happy. Brady's mouth tensed. "Whatever you think, Dad. I'll give him a call Monday morning." More loud conversation from the caller and then Brady said, "All right. I'll get in touch with him today if he's available. Some contractors actually take off on weekends."

He listened a bit longer before hanging up.

"Trouble?" she asked.

"Nothing to worry about." But his light had dimmed and his jaw was tight.

"If you're needed at work…" She gazed around at the activity churning through her house. When the Buchanons started something, they didn't waste time. "This can wait."

"To Dad, work never ends." He winked, but she could see his father had rankled him. "That's where the two of us differ. I take off on Saturdays."

"You call this taking off?"

"This is the fun stuff." He tugged at one of Lila's dog's ears. "I'd better get with it before the others have all the fun without me."

He left them then to help Jake maneuver the refrigerator onto a two-wheel dolly.

By noon, most her belongings had been transferred to storage at the Buchanon Warehouse on the outskirts of town, and her personal items were stacked in cardboard boxes in a spacious bedroom at the Buchanon house.

She stood in the doorway between her room and the adjoining room that would be Lila's. Living with strangers was no big deal to her. She'd done it most of her life. But the Buchanon home felt different than the foster homes she'd bounced in and out of as a teenager. Or maybe she simply wanted it to be different.

The suite off the garage at the back of the house was an addition built for Brady's grandfather and a nighttime caregiver, used now for guests. The house was enormous, at least to her eyes, a sprawling two-story with two living spaces, two dining spaces and more bedrooms than she'd had time to count, all lovingly decorated, as befitted a home builder. And yet, the house felt lived in and comfortable. The night she'd come for dinner, she'd made up her mind to accept Karen's offer the moment she'd walked in the door and Lila had said, "Mommy, it's a castle."

Indeed, the Buchanon home was a castle, and though Abby was embarrassed to accept the help, she wanted her daughter to feel like a princess, at least for a little while.

Brady was feeling pretty good. He'd managed to get his father off his back on Monday morning and the demo bulldozers were on the job at Abby's house by early afternoon. He was too busy with the Huckleberry Creek addition to stop by until after work, but he'd called in some favors to clear the utilities and unhook lines and power, and wrangled the permits out of town hall in record time, thanks to his perfectionist baby sister, Jaylee, who could cut through red tape like a blowtorch. She was office manager to Allison's financial wizardry, two cogs in the mighty Buchanon wheel who kept things turning. Quinn was the grumpy, reluctant architect; the twins computer designed and trimmed out the houses; and Brady served as chief operating officer who could do it all if need be. Charity handled the real estate and Mom designed the landscapes.

Though they employed subcontractors, they remained a family operation where every member played a crucial part. But Dad was the big boss. The big tough boss who saw the problems instead of successes.

The ongoing vandalism on Buchanon Built job sites had them all on edge. The police had yet to come up with a suspect, though nearly a year had passed since the problems began. Trouble didn't happen often, only enough to make them crazy when they let down their guard. Insurance had covered the destruction, but nothing made up for the lost time. Dad had put up a reward for information leading to an arrest but, so far, no takers.

At the row of under-construction homes along Huckleberry Creek, Brady walked through the first nearly finished house, satisfied that they were on schedule. Then he made his way across a wide packed-dirt space that would soon be sodded with grass to house number two. The electrician's van parked on the red dirt yard and ladders leaned against the house indicated work in progress. Brady breathed a sigh of relief. The electrical contractor hadn't been sure he'd be here today. One less thing for Dad to complain about.

He stepped into the structure, smelled the familiar scent of sawdust and drywall mud, Dawg at his heel. An electrician toted a huge reel of cable down the hallway. His assistant poked his head down from the attic and said hello to Brady, then disappeared again.

Brady spoke briefly to the contractor, watched them work for a while and, satisfied everything was going as planned, headed back to his truck. Dad had taken on too many simultaneous projects, at least in Brady's opinion, but he was juggling them all. Something would have to give for him to spend the time on the home makeover, but he'd figure it out. This was the highlight of his year every Christmas and this one seemed even more special than the others.

He didn't question that enthusiasm. Lila and Abby got to him. He liked them, adored Lila and was even starting to enjoy working his way around Abby's defenses. His mother had opened his eyes there. Lacking a family to lean on, Abby had erected a wall of self-sufficiency buttressed with ferocious pride, a wall she didn't need with the Buchanons around, though she probably didn't know that yet.

She was going to love her new home. He'd make sure.

Figuring ten minutes wouldn't make or break him, he drove across the railroad tracks to check on the Cedar Corner demolition. He'd invited Abby to watch, but she'd had to work.

By this time tomorrow, the landscape would be level and ready to start anew. Foundation work could begin immediately. The excitement of a new project all his own revved his engine.

With dust flying amid the dozer's roar, Brady stepped out of his truck to watch the big machine operate.

His father called twice, once to grumble about the substitute plumber he'd hired and once with the good news that the special-order Italian marble had arrived. Jaylee and Charity each texted him a couple of times, and he made eight calls to confirm subcontractors, or subs as he called them, or to line up volunteers for Abby's house, though he planned to do a lot of the work himself. So far, the response had been heartening. His Christmas makeovers were gaining in popularity. Each year, the local newspaper ran a big article, listing all the companies that donated time or materials. Last year, they'd run several, including interviews with the recipients. All of the publicity made his father and the donors happy.

A car pulled alongside his pickup and Abby got out, a hand over her open mouth.

Brady grinned. Watching a demolition was pretty spectacular.

He jogged over to her side. Above the loud engine he shouted, "I thought you had to work."

She crossed her arms over a white button-up sweater. Beneath she wore a Buttered Biscuit T-shirt, though why he'd notice such a thing baffled him.

"I only have an hour. I took a late lunch break so I could take a look."

"Well, what do you think?"

"My house. Oh." Her big brown eyes looked even bigger as she stood in the dust and chill and watched the big machine.

"Is that a good *oh* or a bad *oh*?"

"It's so…permanent."

Were those tears in her eyes?

Alarm pushed Brady into action. "Are you okay? You're not upset, are you?"

"No. Oh, no. This is going to be wonderful."

"Then why the tears?"

"Oh, I'm being sentimental." She patted at her cheeks. "This was the first home that was truly mine."

He studied her features, suddenly seeing the dilapidated old house in a new light. No wonder she'd struggled to let go. As a child of the system, she'd never had a permanent home before.

"You did good, Abby," he said gently, touched. "Real good."

She found a wobbly smile. "Lila and I made a lot of memories here."

Feeling tender, he looped an arm around her shoulders the way he'd do with one of his sisters. "Memories are good. You'll make more in the new place, a home where Lila can grow up and grow strong."

She nodded. "And become independent."

He dipped his head to look at her, saw the hope and longing in her espresso eyes. "Will she?"

"The therapists are always telling me I have to encourage her do more for herself, but it's hard when she can't maneuver the walker farther than the living room. Having a home where she can move more freely, a house with rails and ramps, a lower sink and toilet, will make a world of difference."

Brady's chest expanded. This was why he'd started the Christmas makeovers. There was no feeling as good as this one.

"I have some house plans for you to look at. Mind if I come by later?"

"I get to choose?"

Was she kidding? "Sure. I want you to be happy with the results. It's your house."

She twisted her face toward his and suddenly they were chin to forehead close, and Brady realized his arm was still comfortably wrapped around her shoulders. Nice.

She stared up at him for two beats and must have come to the same realization because she slowly, carefully, edged away. Brady's arm dropped to his side. Abby crossed hers.

He cleared his throat and looked back toward the dozer. The house was now a dusty pile of rubble, and a pair of dump trucks had backed to the site, ready to load up and haul away.

"So, do you want to look at the plans or not?" He sounded gruff and didn't mean to.

"If that's all right with you."

"I wouldn't have asked if it wasn't. My laptop is in the truck if you'd rather take a look now instead of later."

A breeze blew her ponytail across her cheek. She brushed it away. "I have to get back to work."

She backed up two steps, pivoted and walked away. When she reached her car, she turned back. "Brady."

He stuck his hands in his jacket pockets. "Yeah?"

"Thank you."

He dipped his head. "See you later."

After her car chugged down the potholed street, Brady stood in the gray November afternoon strangely discombobulated, and he couldn't for the life of him figure out why.

All afternoon Abby thought of that weird moment when she'd become too aware of Brady's arm around her. He'd meant nothing by it. It was a casual thing. Something he did naturally. He was a man comfortable in his own skin, comfortable with other people, but in that one little moment, his touch had seemed personal. And she'd wanted it to be.

My, but his eyes were blue. And he smelled good even after a busy day on the job.

While she'd served customers and listened to Charla, Jan and Fran the cook discuss the town's Christmas parade and the possibility of opening the Buttered Biscuit afterward for pie and coffee, Brady kept intruding on her thoughts.

She was finally distracted when the bell over the door tinkled and Flo Dubois pranced in on mile-high legs. In tan high-heeled knee boots and cheetah-print leggings, the former Las Vegas showgirl, now in her seventies, retained a flair for the dramatic. Flo stiffened like a cat when she spotted Mayor Hanover perched at the counter reading the newspaper. She marched right up to him and slapped her hand on the paper. The mayor didn't even jump.

He sighed, pushed at his glasses and looked up. "I knew that was you. Could smell the stench of perfume the minute you ripped the door open."

Flo sniffed. "A real man would appreciate it. Which means you don't."

The dozen other customers in the diner quieted, their attention on the mayor and Flo. Abby bussed a suddenly emptied table and wasn't a bit ashamed to have her ears tuned to the entertaining feud. The pair butted heads at least once a week.

"Eau de funeral home," the mayor said. "Flowers and formaldehyde."

Flo rolled her eyes. "New one, Hoss. I suppose you got your nickname from the back end of the equine?"

The mayor sighed. "What do you want now, Flo?"

She smiled a little too sweetly. "So kind of you to ask. As a member of the voting public and a concerned citizen, I want to register a complaint about the trash on Fenton Street and request that something be done about it ASAP. The stink is drawing rats. Which invade homes. Freda Pendleton killed two with a shovel in her front yard."

"Freda did?"

"She did. Bless her heart, and her ninety years old with that awful arthritis having to do such a thing while the mayor is sitting around eating pie. It's a disgrace and a health hazard."

"Couldn't we discuss this in my office?"

"We could if you weren't in here stuffing your face. Funny how I always know where to find you."

He tsked and lifted his fork. "Jealous. Have a bite. It might sweeten you up."

She recoiled as if the fork was a lethal weapon. "I haven't updated my shots."

"Too late. The rabies has already affected your brain. Mouth foaming shall commence. Oh, too late. It already has."

She gave an annoyed huff and flounced. "Are you going to address the situation or not?"

"I'll see what I can do if you promise not to call me for at least a week."

"Promises, my dear mayor, are so pedestrian. Like you." She tossed a mustard-colored scarf over one shoulder, spun on her heel and pranced out as if making an exit in the grand finale at Caesars Palace.

The rest of the time until Abby's shift ended, everyone chattered and chuckled about the latest installment in the continuing saga of Flo and Hoss. Abby and Charla thought they were hilarious. Fran worried about them. But Jan shocked everyone by claiming they were secretly in love and all their gibes were nothing more than a mating ritual.

By the time she'd picked up Lila from day care and headed to the Buchanon house, Abby had put the incident with Brady out of her mind. Mostly.

Nightly dinner with Karen and Dan, which she'd not considered when she'd agreed to camp at their house, was a bonus even if a little on the uncomfortable side at first. The food was far superior to anything she scratched together after work. Karen was a great cook and Abby watched every move she made to learn from her. She'd never known what to do with herbs and seasonings and Karen tossed them around with skill and abandon.

The mealtime prayer had also come as a surprise but Abby kind of liked it, though she knew next to nothing about religion. Only one of her foster families had taken her to church before child services had moved her elsewhere. All she'd learned was the sweetly comforting song, "Jesus Loves Me," which she sometimes sang to Lila. She'd considered attending church for her daughter's sake, but with her work schedule, she'd found Sunday mornings a perfect time to sleep in. The prayer, though, was nice and she felt soothed by Karen's words of faith and grace.

Tonight, the addition of Brady, considering her errant thoughts this afternoon, was both pleasure and discomfort. Sitting on one side of Lila while she sat on the other, he was his usual relaxed self, talking business with his dad, asking his mother about one of his siblings and playing with Lila. She must have imagined that personal moment when he'd looked into her eyes and time had stopped. For her at least. Not for him. Who was she kidding? He'd barely spoken to her since his arrival.

"Will Quinn be here on Sunday?" Brady asked his mother.

Karen frowned down at her chicken piccata, a dish Abby had never heard of until tonight. From all indications, Lila loved the lemony flavor and buttered noodles as much as she did.

"I invited him," Karen said.

"You're worried." Brady's big hands stilled as he looked at his mother.

"I am. Since he moved out of here and into that cabin along the river, he's become more reclusive than he was after the accident."

"I thought he'd put that behind him."

"How can he?" Dan spoke up, his expression hard. "Just because he admitted his culpability in the shooting doesn't mean he isn't permanently handicapped."

At the word *handicapped*, Karen's eyes cut to Lila. Abby carefully put her fork aside. From gossip in the diner she knew the story. Quinn Buchanon had been shot in a hunting accident and the shooter, Jake Hamilton, had been ostracized for years until Quinn had forgiven him and admitted he'd been drinking that day, too. The problem remained, though, that Quinn's professional football career ended on that bloody morning when his throwing arm was forever damaged.

"Dan," Karen said.

"Didn't mean anything by it." He winked at Lila, who beamed, clueless to the undertones about handicaps. Abby wished it could always remain so. "I'm worried about Quinn, too. He does his job at the office, but then he holes up in that cabin like a hermit."

"I tried talking to him," Karen said. "He claims nothing is wrong."

Dan reached for another hot roll. "You don't believe him, do you?"

"Of course not. I know my children." Furrows formed in Karen's forehead, puckering her tidy blond eyebrows. Abby felt awkward at being privy to such a private family conversation, but the Buchanons seemed not to care that she heard. Even successful Christian families like the Buchanons, she saw, had problems. That surprised her, too. She thought Christians had to be perfect.

When dinner ended, Brady helped the women clear the table before heeding his father's call into the living room. Abby organized Lila on a mat with her puzzles in one corner of the kitchen while she assisted with the cleanup. She tried to maintain a low profile and keep Lila out of the Buchanons' way as much as she could. In foster care she'd learned that the less a family noticed her, the longer she got to stay.

Dawg, relegated to the patio during dinner, scratched at the door and whined. Karen let him in. He settled next to Lila without fanfare.

"You don't have to help with cleanup, Abby. You must be worn out from work and you still have Lila's exercises."

"This was part of the deal, remember? I'm okay. Really, and Lila will put off her exercises as long as she can, right, jelly fingers?"

Lila beamed and held up a brown puzzle piece. "Mama, does this piece go there?" She pointed to a spot on the puzzle, clearly an animal, though Abby didn't say so.

"Try and see."

Her face a study in concentration, Lila turned the piece around and around before sliding it into place. "It fits! It's a dog, Mommy, like Dawg."

Dawg put his head in her lap, golden eyes adoring.

"I think you have a friend." Abby retrieved a dishtowel from the cupboard and began drying the dishes too large for the dishwasher.

"He is rather taken with her, isn't he?" Karen's look was amused. "I heard you had an interesting episode today with Mayor Hanover and Flo Dubois."

Abby chuckled. "Oh, that." But before she could rehash the story, raised voices came from the living room.

"I won't put up with slack at the office," she heard Dan say. "None. No concession."

She froze, suddenly wishing she'd made her escape to the bedroom. Conflict stressed her out.

"Buchanon Built has never suffered because of this project. It won't this year, either, Dad. Frankly, I don't know why you're so dead set against something that generates great PR for the company."

Humiliation flushed hot through Abby's body. They were talking about *her*, about the home makeover.

Karen, busy polishing a stainless-steel pot, frowned toward the doorway and clanged the pot onto the counter to cover the conversation. "Don't pay them any mind, Abby. They butt heads all the time."

She'd noticed. But this time the argument was about her.

Chapter Six

"Your dad doesn't want you to build my house."

Abby's blunt statement turned Brady's attention from the stack of floor plans to her face. He could read the hurt and confusion, the embarrassment she tried to hide behind directness.

His temper flared and he battled it down, back teeth tight. No use Abby taking the brunt of his ongoing conflict with his father. Tact was never Dad's strong suit. He should keep his mouth shut.

He and Abby were alone in the breakfast room, thanks to Mom, who'd taken Lila into the family room to watch TV.

"What gave you that idea?"

"I heard." She put her hand over the plans he'd opened on the bar. "I don't know what to do, Brady. My house is gone or I'd walk away from the makeover. The last thing I want is to cause problems for you and your family."

"Stop. Whoa. You are not causing problems. No way. Dad would not want you to think that. I'm sorry if you overheard our discussion, but this is a business issue, a problem between him and me. You have nothing at all to do with it."

"Are you sure?"

He leaned back, looked up at the ceiling and huffed out a breath. Not exactly. Since truth was his method of operation in all things, he admitted, "In the beginning, Dad was against this year's Christmas project. He's usually gung ho, but we've had a rash of vandalism along with the usual problems of running a construction company. Contractors fall behind. Supplies don't come in. Weather delays." He lifted his hands. "Stuff happens. It's the nature of the beast, all of which is my responsibility as chief of operations."

"I've heard about the vandalism. People talk about it at the diner." He saw her glance with longing at the plans.

"Yeah. A real pain in the neck."

"No clues about who's behind it?"

"Nothing that's panned out. We're praying that someone has seen something and will step up with information, but a year has passed and here we are."

He pushed a page of house photos toward her. He had more opened on the laptop if these didn't suit, but they were plans he'd worked with before and could build quickly even with customization.

"Which do you like best? Come on. Stop worrying and get happy. This is supposed to be the part where you get all excited and make me feel like a hero."

Her mouth lifted slightly at his silliness and he felt better. He was still ticked at his father, but that was nothing new.

"I love that one."

"The country cottage?" He'd chosen that one for her the minute he'd seen it. The tidy facade with covered porch, railing, a single dormer and lots of sunny windows was simple and charming. Like her. "Look at the interior plan, too. We can change it around if you like, but the flow is perfect for a walker or a wheelchair. No stairs or ledges. Wide hallways. Lots of storage and cupboards, a safe room and garage."

She studied the plan while he explained each designation and the extras he would add to accommodate Lila's needs. He had a few other extras in mind for Abby, but he was saving those to surprise her.

When he finished, she looked up at him with those soft brown eyes. His chest expanded. She liked it. She liked it a lot. He realized then that he'd been overanxious about this home makeover, afraid she'd regret letting him barge into her life and turn it upside down.

"A safe room, too?"

"This is tornado country. Gotta keep the princess safe. We can add more square footage if you prefer, but the plan has adequate space without making your insurance or utilities too high. I'm thinking cost-effective over the long haul."

"You think of everything, don't you?"

He grinned. "Keep saying things like that and I'll build you the Taj Mahal."

"Who needs the Taj Mahal when this is a dream house, perfect for Lila and me?" She shook her head in wonder. "Is this really going to happen?"

That's the reaction he'd been looking for. "Want to show the princess?"

"She's already so excited she has trouble going to sleep."

"I promised her a princess room."

"She told me. This morning she asked if it was finished yet."

They laughed together in warm affection for the little girl, and once more Brady had the weirdest longing to put his arm around Abby.

"I hope you told her a house takes a little longer than that. If the weather holds so we can complete the exterior and work inside within the next couple of weeks, we're aiming for sixty days, give or take."

Abby looked at him in awe. "That fast?"

"Many hands make light work, remember? We may need longer. Things happen."

"I won't complain no matter how long it takes."

"A Christmas makeover needs to be in progress during the holidays and if we can get close to the finish before New Year's, all the better. The footing crew starts tomorrow morning."

"Tomorrow? Oh, my. I'm overwhelmed. And thrilled. I don't know what to say. None of this seems real."

"Believe it, Abby. It's happening."

Abby was amazed by how soon the house's frame went up and the walls began to take shape. Each day the hours at the diner seemed to creep past before she could rush to the building site to observe the progress. She'd started dreaming, an irresistible by-product. Jan and Charla had gotten in on the excitement by bringing magazines and discussing colors and decor. Brady's mother also fueled the excitement by taking Abby window-shopping the next Saturday afternoon. She didn't have the heart to admit she had no money for extras. Dreaming was fun and she'd almost forgotten how.

Today, when she and Lila arrived, the job site was quiet, completely empty for the first time. Except for a cat sunning on the neighbor's porch with one eye tweaked toward the cardinal hopping around the cluttered lawn, nothing was moving. Yesterday the woman across the street had come over for a look, though because of a language barrier, she and Abby mostly exchanged smiles and charades. Even though Mrs. Herrara seemed genuinely happy for Abby and Lila, the encounter made Abby realize how much a new home would change the look of this tired neighborhood. Sometimes she felt downright guilty for her good fortune.

Often Brady was here when she arrived. When he wasn't,

like today, she suffered a twinge of disappointment, quickly scotched, though Lila was much more vocal.

"Where's Bwady and Dawg?" the four-year-old asked as she peered eagerly through the back car window from her car seat. "Where's his twuck?"

Abby unbuckled her daughter's seat belt. "He must be working somewhere else today."

"But I want to show him my papers." Lila's bottom lip puffed out. "I made him a new picture."

She made him a new picture every single day, and every single day Brady accepted the latest offering as if it was the first and best he'd ever seen.

"Sorry." Stepping carefully around the stacks of lumber debris and packages of shingles that hadn't been here yesterday, Abby and Lila entered the structure. With all the building material around, she carried her child instead of pushing her in the stroller as she did in other situations.

The house was nothing but a frame of concrete and golden wood, but her pulse jumped that she could make out the room divisions. "Look, baby, this is the living room and that will be the kitchen."

"Where's my room?"

"Let's go look." Moving through the space, Lila on her hip, her feet made scratchy sounds against the raw concrete slab as she identified the bedrooms to the left. "One of these will be yours. You can choose which one."

The child blinked in disappointment. "It's not a princess room."

Abby laughed. "Not yet, but it will be."

"And that's a promise." The male voice turned her around. At the sight of Brady, tall and broad, grinning at them from the doorway, her heart leaped with pleasure.

"Hi."

"Bwady!" Lila's greeting was much more effusive. She

waggled her slender arms and Brady swooped her into his. She giggled.

"Hey, squirt. What's shaking?"

"I made you a picture."

"You did? For me?"

There he went again.

Lila beamed. "And guess what?"

"What?" Brady made his eyes wide.

"We had cookies today. Tara bringed them."

"No," he said in mock awe. "What kind?"

"White ones." She nodded in glee. "With chips."

"You're making me hungry. What are your mom and my mom cooking for dinner tonight? I might have to come over."

"I don't know."

He nuzzled her ear, made her giggle and filled Abby with a longing she didn't want. Lila didn't have a man in her life. No dad. No grandpa. No uncles. Abby felt guilty to let her child down in such a fundamentally simple way, though there was nothing she could do to change her empty family tree.

She turned away from the tender sight of big man and tiny girl, arms crossed over her jacket. The weather was cold today, a warning that Mother Nature could interfere with construction anytime she wanted.

"The twins are headed this way. We'll make some progress tonight."

She turned back. "But you've worked all day."

He shrugged. "Is that a problem?"

She supposed not, but if he could do double duty, why couldn't she? "If you'll show me what to do, I'll help."

"Nah, we got this."

Her shoulders tightened. "Sweat equity, Brady. I want to. In fact, I insist."

Brady studied her for several seconds and she could see

the wheels turning behind his blue, blue eyes. Foolishly, she wondered how many women had gone gaga over those thick-lashed eyes?

"There are always odds and ends a layman can do, but why not wait until we're working inside. Evenings get pretty cool."

"They aren't going to get warmer."

"Once the house is enclosed, the weather won't be a factor."

"What are you working on tonight?"

"Decking." He pointed upward at the empty space where a roof would be. "Sheets of plywood for the roof base. We should be able to knock that out tonight."

"I can use a hammer. I fixed the shingles on the old house." She didn't add how nervous heights made her or how her stomach dipped anytime she stood on a ladder. A girl did what a girl had to do.

"We've put up decking so often we're really fast."

"In other words, I'll be in the way?"

He squeezed her upper arm between his finger and thumb, a gentle touch. "Give us another week or two to get the rough work finished. After that, there'll be plenty for you to do."

Though she didn't want him to know he was winning or how relieved she was not to get on the roof, she nodded. "Okay, that makes sense."

Car doors slammed and Brady looked through the framing toward the lawn. "Sawyer and Dawson are here."

"My cue to leave. Your mother will be wondering where we are." Her cell, as usual, was out of minutes.

She took Lila from him and headed toward the exit.

"Go feed the princess."

She glanced over one shoulder. "What about you?"

"I'll grab something later."

He was planning to work half the night on an empty stomach?

Abby thought about his words until she reached the car. He'd told her once before he required plenty of fuel for that big body of his. She may not be able to help with the house just yet, but she could definitely help with food.

Brady heard her pull up, recognizing the car by the engine clatter. Like her former home, the car was nearing the end of its long life.

From his spot on top of the house, he saw Abby's dome light illuminate, saw her hop out of the car. In the shadowy glow of halogen floodlights he'd set up in the front yard, she waved. "Are you guys hungry?"

Dawson, nail gun rat-a-tatting, stopped nailing long enough to call, "You brought food?"

"From your mom's kitchen."

"I'm starving." To his brothers, Dawson said, "You?"

Both men nodded.

In seconds, the three had cast aside their tools and descended the ladder.

"You didn't have to do this," Brady said. His belly growled at the smells coming out of his mom's picnic basket. "I could have grabbed a sandwich when I got home."

Abby had tossed on a coat, a parka that had seen better days, but the red color turned her dark hair to ebony in the dim lighting.

She hoisted the basket and said, "Delivering plates is what I do. I'm pretty good at it."

He frowned. "You don't have to wait on us like a servant."

Sawyer elbowed him. "Lighten up, brother. She brought food. Mama's food."

Dawson rubbed his hands together. "What are we having?"

"Roast pork tenderloin, new potatoes and green beans. Chocolate cake for dessert."

All three men moaned in appreciation. "Bring it on!"

The temperature had dropped with the sun, so they piled into the back of the company work van and sat among tools and compressors. Brady was accustomed to eating wherever he could on a job site, but this time he found a mostly clean drop cloth and spread it in the open space between a table saw and several five-gallon buckets.

"Elegant," Dawson said, teasing as he settled on one of the buckets.

Brady shot him a glower. "There's a lady present. We don't have to be slobs."

Dawson and Sawyer traded amused glances. Brady knew they had some kind of silent twin communication thing going on. They always had. But this time, the glances went from him and Abby to each other. Then Sawyer gave a nod and they both twitched an eyebrow.

Were they talking about him? And Abby? Brady wouldn't ask now, but he *would* ask.

"Where's the princess?" He took the plate Abby offered and parked his big body on the drop cloth.

"Asleep in the backseat. It's nearing her bedtime, so the drive did her in."

He glanced toward the car, parked a short distance behind the van. "Is she okay out there?"

"Snug and warm, but I'll be checking on her."

"You could have left her with Mom."

"I wouldn't impose like that. It's enough that your parents are giving us a place to stay. I don't expect free babysitting service. With my work schedule and day care, I like to have Lila with me as much as possible anyway." From a thermos, she poured cups of coffee and passed them around. "How are things coming?"

"Decking's almost finished. Then the moisture barrier.

That goes on fast. If this good weather holds, we'll make some serious progress this weekend."

"Exciting."

"Isn't it?" He liked hearing her say that. "Feel free to watch anytime."

"And help."

He jabbed a piece of tenderloin. He admired her spunk, her determination, and if assisting with the house would make her feel better, he'd find some little task for her to do. Something easy and not too taxing. She worked hard enough as it was.

"So you said. Are you working at the diner this weekend?"

"I'm off the next three days. Tomorrow Lila has her appointments."

"With the doctor?" He paused, fork in midbite. "Is she okay?"

"The usual. Therapists, doctors. The plan of action for the next six months." Abby ran a finger over the rim of her mug. "She'll have a blood draw and other tests. Those are not fun."

"Yeah, I guess not. I'll pray she handles it okay." He offered a smile. "That both of you do."

As though she didn't know how to respond, Abby blinked at the declaration. Hadn't anyone ever prayed for her before?

"Oh…well…thanks."

He hadn't intended to make her uncomfortable, but apparently faith was an area where he'd have to walk softly and pray hard.

"Did you see the picture she gave me today?"

Abby shook her head. "Another angel?"

"A pink angel with wings…and a walker."

"Oh. Oh, my baby." Abby's expression melted, and Brady fought the urge to draw her into a hug. The last time he'd put his arm around her, something weird had happened. With his workload, he didn't need weird in his life right now.

He tapped his heart. "Yeah. Got me right there. What a little champ."

"She's a trouper. No matter what the therapists ask her to do, she perseveres. I wish her life could be easier. She's such a great kid with a terrific attitude and sunny personality. I worry the obstacles of spina bifida will eventually beat her down."

She worried a lot. He'd seen that as he'd gotten to know her better. He didn't like that she worried so much, though in her situation raising a child alone, especially a child with unending medical needs, who could blame her?

He stopped short of asking about Lila's father. Too personal. With his temper he might have to punch someone and he hadn't done that since he'd fully committed his life to Christ. Not that his temper had suddenly disappeared. He was simply better at handling it.

Once again, he resisted the urge to touch her, jabbing at a green bean instead. "She can't fail. She's got you for a mother."

Suddenly, her eyes got all shiny as if she was going to cry. She turned aside and scrambled to her feet. "I should take a peek at her. Be right back."

She hopped out of the van and slammed the door before he could react.

Brady stared at the closed door. "I didn't mean to upset her."

"I don't think you did." Sawyer made a humming noise. "I like her, too."

"Not the way Brady does, I hope," Dawson said. "I wouldn't want your pretty face getting smashed up."

Brady chewed a buttery potato, swallowed and growled at his dimpled brother. "What are you two muttering about?"

"You and Abby sound pretty cozy. I think you completely forgot about Sawyer and me."

He had. "Don't be stupid."

Sawyer laughed and whacked him on the shoulder. "Go ahead and finish your dinner, old man. Dawson and I can nail those last couple of sheets on before we hit the road."

Brady stared at his half-finished plate. How had they eaten so fast and he had so much left? Had he really been that engrossed in the conversation with Abby? "I'll be up in a minute."

"Take your time."

He tossed back the rest of his coffee, zipped his jacket and followed his brothers back up on the roof. Time was a commodity he couldn't waste.

Chapter Seven

Abby's usually dependable, ancient Honda wouldn't start.

Shivering against the early-morning chill, Abby ground the starter. After a few sluggish chugs, the thing clicked twice and went silent.

"Battery," she muttered. Or starter or alternator or… something. She didn't have time for this today, not with the hospital an hour away and Lila's appointments at nine.

"Mommy, are we going?" Lila, bundled in her car seat in back, peered out from a pink hood.

"I hope so." With shoulders slumped, Abby stared at the windshield while she tried to figure out her next move. The Buchanons had already left for work, not that she would have asked. As she contemplated going back inside to phone a mechanic, a big blue Ford rumbled up behind her.

Brady hopped out and came to the window. His breath blew vapor into the chill. "I thought you might already be gone."

"I would have been if my car would start."

His eyebrows came together in a frown. "Pop the hood."

She did. He poked his head inside the workings of the Honda. "Crank it."

She did. A few clicks later, he slammed the hood and

came around. "Probably your battery. This time of year, a weak one gives it up on the first cold morning. I could give you a jump, but I don't think it's a good idea for you to drive that far until a mechanic has a look."

"I have to."

"No, you don't. I'll take you. Hop in the truck. I'll get the princess."

Abby was already shaking her head. "No, Brady. Thank you for the offer, but we'll be gone most of the day. You're too busy for that."

"A man who's too busy to help a friend is too busy." He opened Lila's door and reached inside, unhooked the car seat and lifted Lila, seat and all, out into the morning. She giggled and patted his face.

Abby sighed. As usual, she didn't have much choice. Coordinating all of Lila's appointments in one day required extra time and effort from the doctors and therapists. Canceling was not a good option.

"Do you always get your way?" she asked, making one last attempt.

He already had Lila in the crew cab, buckled in with paper and markers and a new coloring book in hand. "Time's wasting."

Suffering deeper feelings of obligation, Abby grabbed Lila's backpack and climbed into the cab.

Brady pulled onto the highway and headed toward the regional medical clinic an hour away. Abby was right. He didn't have time for this. But he wasn't about to tell her that. She had enough trouble accepting a simple act of kindness. For some reason, she couldn't get it through her head that friends helped friends. It was the Buchanon way.

He'd made a few calls from his truck's Bluetooth, rearranged some appointments and let the office know he was out of pocket for the day. He was sorry about making the calls in front of Abby because she'd slumped farther into her seat with each one.

"I've caused you too much trouble," she said when he completed the final call.

"Don't worry about it." The rest he could manage on his smartphone while he waited at the hospital.

"Why did you come by this morning anyway? Or are you just especially unlucky?" She had her arms crossed, a sign she was uncomfortable. He wanted to change that but didn't know how.

"Mom asked me to drop off a coloring book for Lila on the long ride."

"Your mother is incredibly thoughtful. So are you."

He lifted his fingers from the steering wheel, ignoring the compliment. "What's the itinerary today?"

She went through a litany of doctors, tests, therapists and meetings. "Sometimes we stay on schedule, sometimes not. I'm hoping this time will go fast."

"I've never known anyone with spina bifida before." He glanced in the rearview. "Is it okay to talk about it in front of her?"

Abby nodded. "I'm careful with what I say, but she knows even though she's still too young to understand what the diagnosis means for her future. This is her normal."

Her normal. The truth pinched him. Lila had never known any way other than her physical impairment. But someday, when she was older, she'd notice the things other kids did that she couldn't.

He glimpsed the mirror again, saw Lila's eyes drooping. In a minute, she'd be fast asleep. He kept his voice low just the same. "What *does* the future hold?"

Abby hitched one shoulder. "No one can predict. We were fortunate that the spinal cord opening was down low on her spine and not on the outside. Because of that, she has greater nerve development than most spina bifida patients. But still, some kids with her exact diagnosis never walk and some don't seem to have any disability at all." She lifted her palms. "Every child with a neural-tube defect is different."

Neural tube defect. She was talking over his head. His degree was in business, not medicine. "You talk like a doctor."

"I've lived and breathed her diagnosis for a long time, Brady. I had to educate myself for her sake. The more I know, the more I can help her."

Chalk another one up for Abby Webster. Impressive woman. "What causes spina bifida? Or is it one of those mysteries?"

"No one knows for certain." She lowered her eyes and fidgeted with her thumbnail. "There are risk factors, like low levels of folic acid in the mother."

He glanced toward the highway and back to her. "You feel responsible?"

"That I might have done something to hurt my baby? I'd never heard of folic acid before I had Lila, but if I'd taken it, she'd probably be fine. Now, she struggles to walk, struggles with toilet training. She can't even climb a playground slide. Everything is a struggle for her. She's endured four surgeries and will likely have more." She blinked shiny eyes. "Of course, I feel guilty."

Brady reached across the bucket seat to squeeze Abby's hand. "Don't. Lila's blessed to have you."

"I'm the one who's blessed," she said softly, and then turned her face toward the passenger window and the miles of yellowing grass and piney woods.

The cab grew silent, and deep in thought, Brady clicked on the radio. He had a feeling he was about to get a life lesson from one sunny, tough little girl with something called spina bifida…and her equally strong mother.

The following Sunday, Abby attended church with the Buchanons, the day she'd spent with Brady at the hospital heavy on her mind and heart. The truth was, she'd thought of little else, of his compassion, his consideration and the way he'd dumped his schedule to drive them. She wasn't accustomed to anyone going out of his way for her. As nice as it was, she questioned his motives. Why would he do that? What would he want in return?

Whatever the price, Brady's company had been worth it. He'd made the usually grueling day almost enjoyable. Lila, determined to be brave in front of her hero, had basked in his attentions and sailed through most of her tests with a smile.

Today was Abby's first time attending church in years and she'd come mostly to please Karen. How could she refuse after all they'd done for her? Seeing Brady again was an added bonus.

The Buchanons, she discovered with amusement, required two pews. The only one missing was Dan who'd decided to work today, and Abby found herself wedged between Karen and Brady. Brady cleaned up really well, as if he wasn't already good-looking enough. In dark slacks, white shirt and a blue tie that matched his eyes, he looked as good as he smelled, which was delicious.

All during the worship service, while the music director led them in songs she didn't know, Brady shared his hymnal. He had a pleasant voice and she mouthed the words to hear him better.

And if the image of this giant man holding her baby girl on the slide at McDonald's played in her head, she couldn't help it.

After a woman made announcements, the pastor spoke.

Abby was prepared to be bored, but the message was surprisingly simple and relevant, and she found herself listening with interest. He spoke of a father's love for his child, something she didn't know anything about, but when he spoke of the breakdown in families that damage the father-child relationship, she knew exactly what he meant.

"Some of your earthly fathers may have been absent or they may have disappointed you or hurt you or let you down too many times to trust them," he said. "But God is a Father you can depend on. He is a compassionate and merciful Father who wants to be there for you always, to heal your hurts and guide your steps every day of your life." The minister lifted his hands, palms up as if holding something in each. "The choice to be a greatly loved child of God is yours. The Father waits with arms outstretched."

Abby got a lump in her throat when he said the last. She'd never had a father's embrace and remembered movies in which the child ran into her father's arms for a hug. Sometimes she fantasized about being that child.

Would her daughter feel the same someday?

Surrounded by Buchanons and with Brady's arm brushing hers, Abby couldn't help dreaming of a father and a family for her little girl.

At the end of the service while the piano played softly, the minister asked if anyone needed prayer. She recalled Brady's offer to pray for Lila and her. Prayer. She'd given it little thought. Did praying really do anything?

So many questions and feelings swirled inside as she left the church and got into the car with Karen for the trip home.

"Did you enjoy the service?" Karen asked from her spot behind the steering wheel.

"I think so."

Karen laughed before sobering. "Was something wrong?"

She turned in the seat. "It all seems too good to be true."

"What does?"

"A loving Father who forgives you for all the rotten things you've done and never stops loving you. Why would He do that?"

"That's where Jesus comes in, honey. The Father loved us so much He allowed His son to die in our place. If He was willing to do that, His love must be pretty big."

"It sounds like a fairy tale."

Karen was quiet for a moment before saying, "I grew up without a father, too, Abby."

"I didn't know that."

"My dad died in an oil field accident when I was three." Karen clicked on the signal light and turned at the stop-light. "I struggled to comprehend a father who could love me, a father who wasn't absent, but once I became a child of the King, oh, honey, I can't tell you what a huge hole in my soul Jesus has filled."

"Did you grow up around Christians?"

"No, I didn't. My mom hated God because she blamed Him for the loss of my dad. I was scared of God, afraid He'd kill me or someone else I loved." She pulled the car into the garage and stopped. "I was terribly wrong. That's not who God is, Abby. God is for us, not against us."

Abby said nothing but she absorbed Karen's words to ponder. She'd always thought of God, when she thought of Him at all, as an invisible being who didn't care, like her earthly father. Or if He noticed her at all, it was to pass judgment on her misbehavior. *God will get you*, she'd heard people say.

She exited the car, unstrapped Lila. Karen came around to her side, house keys in hand.

"Thank you," Abby said.

Karen cocked her head. "For?"

"Answering my dumb questions."

"Questions are never dumb. Ask me anything, anytime." She unlocked the door and pushed it open. "Smell that soup. Is that delicious or what?"

"Is everyone coming over for dinner?" Abby shifted Lila to her opposite hip, trying to pretend she wasn't asking specifically about Brady.

"I'm hungry, Mama."

"You're always hungry, jelly fingers."

Karen opened the pantry and handed out a pack of gummy fruits. "Will these hold you until dinner?"

"Yummy!"

"What do you say?"

"Thank you vewy, vewy much."

The mothers exchanged smiles.

"The whole gang will show up before the day is over. The Cowboys don't play until tomorrow night, but my bunch will gather for anything that involves the three F's—family, food and football." On chunky heels, Karen tapped over the tile to peer in the oven. "I hope you like noisy crowds."

She worked in a diner. It couldn't be any noisier or more crowded than the noon rush.

She was wrong.

Sunday afternoon proved to the wildest, noisiest time Abby had witnessed in years. The four Buchanon males, their three sisters, kids she'd never seen and couldn't remember, and a couple of extra guys, including Jake Hamilton, roamed through the kitchen and living areas in friendly arguments about Fantasy Football teams while stuffing their faces. Everyone brought something. Pizza, buffalo wings, chips, dips, and a huge veggie and fruit tray contributed by one of the sisters, Jaylee, the only one who seemed concerned about carbs or processed foods and who made a point of reminding her brothers that chips and dip would clog the arteries and lead to a sure death. The men were not in the least deterred.

They all talked at once, hooting and laughing at the TV or something one of them said. Abby's head swam from the sheer energy of the group.

And Brady. She couldn't keep her eyes off him.

"It's a party. It's a party!" Lila said, and giggled when Brady pointed his big index finger at her and winked.

"Sure it is, squirt. Come here and I'll teach you about football. All you need to know is that the linebacker is the man!"

Lila pulled her walker as close as she could to her adored Bwady. So many legs sprawled across the floor, she couldn't maneuver through. Sawyer, the closest to her, saw the dilemma and shouted, "Handoff."

He scooped her up in his strong carpenter's hands, lifted her high over his head and passed her to Dawson, who handed her to Brady. Lila's giggle rang out, sweet and joyous.

"You boys," Charity said with a head shake.

"Again, again," Lila cried.

"Lila," Abby said. "Don't be a pest."

"Sowwy." She hung her head.

"Hey, no sad faces." Brady tugged gently on one of her twin ponytails, grinning. "Santa Claus might be watching."

"Really?" Lila perked up and glanced around the room. "Mommy, guess what?"

"What?" Abby leaned against the doorway between kitchen and family room, smiling at her daughter's pleasure and at the sweetness of her interaction with Brady.

The need for family pulled at her.

"Santa Claus is coming."

"Won't be long."

"Tomorrow?"

"Not that soon. Thanksgiving comes first."

Karen poked her head into the room. "Is everyone going to be here on Thanksgiving? Jake, did you remember to invite your grandmother?"

Jake waved one hand. "Done. She said she'd pencil it on her social calendar but if the governor called, she'd have to cancel."

They all chuckled. Granny Pat, best friend to Flo Dubois, was as sassy as her friend, though her health had deteriorated in recent years and, like Lila, she used a walker for mobility.

Allison, lounging close to her cowboy, patted the opposite side of the couch. "Come sit down, Abby, if you can tolerate my brothers. There's room."

Abby did as she asked, pleased to be included. She didn't say much, but she smiled a lot and laughed at the interactions between the siblings. She listened to their snatches of conversation, both teasing and serious, if listening was possible when everyone talked at once and the big screen blared. They were wonderful, happy, loving, a family like she'd never witnessed before. A hot balloon of emotion expanded in her chest, a chasm of need so deep and wide as to make her eyes misty.

She blinked away the moisture.

Being with the Buchanons was both overwhelming and fulfilling. And if she found herself focused more on Brady and listening to him talk, it was because she knew him best. That was all. This silly schoolgirl crush would subside when the house was finished. She knew better than to let that kind of emotion get out of hand.

At halftime of the game between Arizona and Denver, the five males trotted into the backyard to throw a worn football around while the women discussed the upcoming Thanksgiving meal and Black Friday shopping.

Brady's father still had not returned from work, and

Abby found it interesting that he was the only Buchanon not fully committed to church and Sundays off.

After a bit, the men swarmed into the kitchen like a biblical plague to gorge on more food and claim victory.

Brady, sipping Coke from a can, reached for a slice of apple. His cell phone jangled. He stuffed the apple in his mouth, set the Coke aside and answered.

"Dad, what's up?" he said, around the bite of apple. "Yeah, yeah, everyone's here. Why don't you knock off work and come home for the second half? It's a pretty good game."

Whatever Dan replied erased Brady's cheerful expression. His next words were too low for Abby to hear, but they were short and crisply spoken.

He tapped the screen and rang off, staring down at the phone for a couple of seconds.

"What is it, son?" Karen asked. "Not another break-in."

"No." He blew out a sigh. "Dad thinks he needs my input."

"Can't it wait until tomorrow?"

"Apparently not." He pocketed the cell.

"Want us to come along?" Dawson asked. He popped open a bag of tortilla chips.

"Nah. I got this." Brady play-punched his brother's arm. "Keep the party going. I shall return."

The afternoon wasn't as much fun after he left.

Thanksgiving proved to be a bigger, noisier version of Sunday afternoons. Abby worried about intruding on a family event and worried even more about Lila being in the way, particularly when Dan was home. Even though Brady's dad was cordial, he made her nervous. She'd heard his harsh tone with Brady and she didn't like it.

But when Thanksgiving Thursday arrived, she and Lila weren't the only non–family members invited to the Buchanon feast. Several men and women Abby had seen on the construction site joined Jake and Pat Hamilton and a half dozen unfamiliar kids who ran in and out of the house with Dawg.

Inside the kitchen, Abby helped the others organize the enormous number of casseroles and desserts while Brady and Dan carved up two turkeys and a ham, joking about who was the best carver and chuckling over Samurai warrior jokes from a TV show. Abby watched, puzzled and intrigued that two men who could be at odds one day were clearly having a good time together.

The inner workings of a big family, particularly this one, bewildered her.

Lila tried to keep up with the other children on her walker but failed and ended up standing at the patio door watching the game of tag. The sight made Abby's heart heavy. Without being obvious, Abby observed her daughter, all the while wondering what she could do to make up for Lila's lack of playmates. She was never one to ask for special privileges or attention, even for Lila.

Brady's niece, Amber, pressed her face against the glass of the patio doors. She was a cute thing, blond as her mother with a tilted nose and blue eyes. Her gaze lit on Lila and she grinned, showing an empty space where her front teeth had been. She slid open the glass door, letting in a waft of cold air and said to Lila, "I brought my dolls. Want to play with me?"

Abby's heavy heart lifted even as tears of gratitude stung her eyes.

Lila's face lit up. "Okay."

Amber shed her jacket, letting it drag behind her as she took two steps toward the living room, then turned to watch Lila's progress. "I'll wait for you."

Abby's chest squeezed with gratitude as Charity's little girl patiently strolled alongside the walker, one hand on

Lila's back as if to assist. Lila, her face set in concentration and determination, maneuvered across the room and down the hall.

Abby caught Charity's eye over the bar piled with food. "Your little girl has a kind heart. You should be proud."

"I am." Charity's smile was soft as her gaze followed the two girls. "Her daddy and I live for moments like this. Lila is a sweetheart, too. She's easy to like."

Pleasure ballooned inside. "Thank you."

Charity moved a chocolate pie to the dessert table and reached for a coconut cream with sky-high meringue. "What's the latest report on your house? Brady seems supercharged this year about the project."

Supercharged. "Isn't he always?"

Charity chuckled. "Oh, sure. He's a regular Santa at Christmas, the big teddy bear, but I don't know, he seems more excited about your house for some reason."

"Probably because he's building from the ground up instead of remodeling." It couldn't be anything else. "We're in the dry now, as he calls it. I'm impressed at how fast his crew can build."

"They are pretty impressive." She leaned closer. "Dawson thinks Brady has his eye on you."

Heat flushed Abby's neck. She opened a drawer in search of a serving spoon. "Dawson likes to kid around."

Guys like Brady Buchanon didn't look twice at girls from the wrong side of the tracks except when that particular girl was his latest charity project.

Charity tilted her head, eyebrows knit together. "Brady's a good guy. Don't you like him?"

Like him? She was smitten with all six-and-a-half feet of him. "He's been very kind to us."

Before Charity could embarrass her more, Dan's voice boomed across the room. "Listen up, folks. Heads bowed. We're going to say grace and let the games begin."

After a round of *shh*, silence fell on the house like a curtain and Dan spoke a simple prayer.

"Thank You, Heavenly Father, for this incredible feast you've provided. Thank You, too, that this family could once more gather as a whole to celebrate this day, and thank You, Father, for our blessings of this year and for the guests who've come to share those blessings. Through Jesus we pray. Amen."

It was simple, heartfelt and as foreign to Abby as this Thanksgiving dinner. The only big holiday meals she'd attended had been held by social services for foster kids. They were nice, but not like this, not family.

"Buffet style, y'all." Karen circled a finger around the tables and counters of food. "Everything is organized by type. Salads there. Meats here. Side dishes and casseroles over here. Grab a plate and help yourself."

The long dining table filled in minutes and the overflow sat at the bar and at a pair of folding tables stretched as far as the family room. Succulent scents floated into Abby's senses as she filled Lila's plate and sat her daughter in a booster chair at one of the folding tables dubbed the kids' table. She didn't know what was wrong with her today, but she got teary when Amber and another little girl parked on each side of Lila and stared to chatter.

"Looks like you've been demoted," Brady said as his big body maneuvered through the crowd of plate fillers.

Abby blinked away the unusual tears. She wasn't a crier—life had taught her that crying didn't do a bit of good and often made things worse—but, lately, her emotions were too close to the surface.

"I'm glad. She's having fun with the girls today. Your niece is a sweetie."

He reached around her for a chunk of turkey and a bigger chunk of ham. "Aren't you going to eat?"

"If you leave me any of that turkey." Her sassy answer

caught her off guard. She was not one to joke around, even at the diner. These lighthearted Buchanons were having a strange effect on her.

Brady stabbed another piece of turkey and dropped it on her plate. "There you go. How about some stuffing?"

She took the spoon from him. "I'm a big girl, but this piece of turkey is enough for a week."

He grinned and jerked his head toward the table. "Fill 'er up. I'll save you a seat."

He would? Pulse thrumming a little erratically, Abby helped herself to the abundant meal. Brady topped his plate with two steaming hot rolls and moved away. She took her time, trying to get a handle on the emotion dancing around in her chest. Brady meant nothing by the saved seat. He was being hospitable, friendly, making a stranger feel welcome. She really needed to stop overreacting to kindness just as she needed to get a handle on this stupid crush.

When her plate was filled, she avoided looking toward Brady's table, choosing instead an empty chair next to Jaylee. When she saw the tiny amount of food on the woman's plate, she regretted her decision. Svelte and diet-conscious Jaylee made her feel like an Amazon. A gluttonous Amazon.

But sitting with a thin, beautiful Buchanon was better than making a fool of herself by chasing after the handsome giant Buchanon. They passed the meal in pleasant conversation, mostly about the town's upcoming Christmas parade and chocolate festival and tomorrow's Black Friday sales ads.

"Do you want to go with us, Abby?" Jaylee dipped her fork into a tiny portion of cranberry salad.

The invitation caught Abby off guard. "Oh, no thank you. I don't think so."

"You don't know what you're missing. We have a blast and find a lot of bargains in the process."

"Charity maps out a plan." Allison leaned around her fiancé, her fork filled with baked-potato casserole. "Then the four of us split up, using our cell phones to text or pix a bargain we find."

"It's so much fun," Jaylee said. "Afterward, we meet up for a late breakfast and share our treasures. A real girls' day out."

"Exhausting and exhilarating, especially when one of us snags a limited-supply item. You should hear the squealing, in text format, of course." A piece of pumpkin pie in hand, Karen had stopped at their table. She smiled at the last statement. "We'd love to have you come along."

It did sound fun, but her budget couldn't manage much this year and she didn't want to embarrass herself in a group of free spenders.

Abby reached for her tea glass. "You're nice to ask, but I'll be working at the house tomorrow."

Now that the house was enclosed, she spent every extra minute there. Often Brady or the twins were the only ones working and she'd quickly learned to run a sander and a nail gun.

"I don't blame you one bit, Abby," Karen said. "A new house is even more fun than a wild spree with the Buchanon girls. Let us know if there is anything in the ads we can pick up for you."

"I—haven't had a chance to look." She hadn't planned to look. Looking led to longing.

"What does Lila want for Christmas?" Allison glanced toward the little girls.

"We really haven't talked about it. We're both too excited about the house. That's our Christmas present this year."

Her statement moved the conversation to the makeover, which made Abby about as uncomfortable as the topic of Christmas presents. She was thrilled over the house, truly she was, but being the focus of the Buchanons' altruism at the dinner table drove home the fact that she and Lila were a charity case, not family like the rest.

Later that afternoon, when guests had departed and only the family remained, Karen stepped in front of the television with an announcement. "Who's going to help put up the tree?"

When Abby glanced at Allison, she explained, "Thanksgiving evening is our traditional day to put up the decorations."

"That's because she has all of us corralled," Sawyer said, grinning.

"You got that right. Sawyer, you and Dawson can start on the outside lights," Karen ordered like a general. "Brady and Dan, if you'll get the tree out of storage, the girls and I will find the decorations."

"What about us, Nana? We want to help?" This from Amber, who bounced up and down in excitement at the mention of a Christmas tree.

"You, my little sugarplum," Karen said, tapping Amber's pert nose, "along with your brother and Lila will be my very special helpers. Brady, turn the channel to Sounds of the Season."

The men groaned good-naturedly. "Mom and her Christmas music." To Abby, Quinn said, "Prepare to be driven crazy for the next few weeks."

Karen's laughter rang out. "Don't complain. Santa is watching."

Dawson looped an arm over his mother's shoulders much the way Brady had once done to Abby. Casual. Affectionate. "She used to torture us with that dire warning when we were kids."

"Yeah," Sawyer said. "If Dawson and I got in a disagreement, which might have happened pretty often, we were doomed to nothing but twigs in our stockings and no visit from Saint Nick."

"It worked, didn't it?" Karen patted her son on the very flat belly. "You boys were good as gold from Thanksgiving until Christmas."

"After that, the deal was off." Dawson feigned a punch at his twin. "Hammer time."

"We weren't as bad as Brady," Sawyer said. "He had to hold his temper for an entire month even when we pestered him and snitched his stuff without permission."

Brady pointed at his brother. "You knew I couldn't retaliate."

"Exactly. Santa Claus was watching." Sawyer's grin spread across his face. "We thought you might explode."

Amidst the good-natured family reminisces, the tall, artificial pine went up in the family room. The Buchanons pulled her in, handing her ornaments to hang and asking her opinion. Lila helped Amber place small golden bells on the lower branches and no one seemed to mind the uneven clumps of bells and empty spaces the girls created. With a thick ache in her chest, Abby watched her child be swept into the wonder and warmth of a big family.

The longing grew to such intensity that when the room was darkened and the tree twinkled merrily, Abby slipped away to the new house with Lila. Being with the Buchanons too much caused her to dream of things she'd never had and never would.

Chapter Eight

Abby had ditched him.

The next day, as Brady pulled into the home makeover site, his ego still smarted from yesterday's dinner. She'd rejected his offer to sit together even though he'd saved her a chair next to his, an act that had brought comments from his brothers, especially when she'd chosen to sit with his sisters, instead. And during the time they'd put up the lights and tree, she'd not said one word to him. Not one.

He'd thought they were... He wasn't sure what they were. Friends, at least. On the cold, gray day he'd driven her and Lila to the medical center, a subtle shift had occurred in their relationship. At least for him.

He thought about that day a lot. He'd never imagined the amount of tests and exams one small child would have to endure. Lila had cried a couple of times and Brady had wanted to hit something. Instead, he'd given her piggyback rides up and down the corridor, made her giggle and promised lunch at her favorite eating place.

But the real kicker had been afterward. Instead of heading home, they'd visited the pediatric wing, where Lila had dragged her walker from room to room to distribute her brand of cheer and hand-drawn angel cards to sick kids. As if she didn't have problems of her own.

Abby was a great mother, as strong and resilient as her daughter, and he'd admired the way she interacted with the medical team, absorbing advice and adding her own. He'd seen the tears she hid from her daughter. They'd ripped him in half.

So, yeah. When he considered that day, along with the time they spent on the house and the family gatherings, he thought Abby liked him. They talked and laughed over silly things at the building site, shared a love of country music, polished wood, fried cherry pies. They were friends, weren't they?

Okay, he got the message. He hadn't meant anything romantic when he'd invited her sit with him anyway. At least, he didn't think so. He simply hadn't wanted her to feel alone and out of place in the sometimes overwhelming Buchanon household. He'd had girlfriends who'd felt that way.

At the thought of girlfriends, he paused. Abby was not a girlfriend although they spent a lot of time together. Especially lately, since she'd become as much a crew member as some of his professional volunteers. He liked her, wouldn't mind hanging out more, and he got this little hum of energy under his skin whenever he saw her.

Having her and Lila present during the tree decorating had given an extra zing to the family tradition. And maybe he'd glanced her way a few too many times. Her look of wonder and pleasure had matched that of the children, and she'd hummed along with Mom's Christmas carols.

So yeah, he wouldn't mind getting cozy with Abby Webster. She, apparently, was not on the same page.

She was, however, inside the house when he turned the knob and stepped inside. They were insulating and he could hear her dragging fiberglass batting across the concrete, alone except for Lila. He'd balked at first about having a toddler on the job site, but Abby insisted. So, after the heating unit had gone live, he'd cleared out a space in one of the soon-to-be bedrooms, where Lila could play safely while the adults worked.

And, man, did Abby work. She'd stand on her feet for ten hours at the diner and then show up on the job immediately after and labor until midnight. She had to be exhausted but if she was, she wouldn't let anyone know. She just kept on working.

A man had to admire a woman like her.

"Hey," he said, entering the master bedroom. Abby stood on a stepladder pressing insulation into the spaces between the two-by-sixes.

Her head swiveled toward him. She tugged down the yellow particle mask he'd insisted she wear. "Hey, yourself."

"I see you remembered your safety glasses."

She made a face, her dark eyes even more enormous behind the plastic goggles. "My big mean boss threatened to fire me if I didn't wear them."

"He's a slave driver." With a smile, he leaned a shoulder against the open door facing. "Where'd you run off to yesterday?"

One minute they'd been decorating the tree and the next she and Lila were gone. Even Dad had noticed the departure and wondered if someone had upset her.

"Take a look at the master bathroom."

He stuck his head inside the adjoining space. "Did you do all that by yourself?"

Her smile was bright. She always lit up like Gabriel's Crossing's Christmas tree whenever he paid her a compliment. "Will you check to see if everything is done right?"

"We thought you might be upset about something."

"Why would you think that?"

"You left early. Kind of abruptly. We wondered." Actually, he'd wondered more than anyone.

"We loved yesterday. Really. I am simply too excited about the house to stay away."

Okay, that made sense. His mood elevated as he stepped into the other room and flipped on the light. Pink batting lined the walls in a tight configuration. He walked around the room, tugged on the batting here and there, checked the rough-in electric outlets for a tight fit.

She must have stayed half the night to finish this alone. And yesterday was Thanksgiving, a day to kick back. Except for Abby. He should have known she'd come here.

He returned to the master bedroom. "Great job, Ab. You're hired."

She beamed again and he got a weird swoopy feeling in his belly.

"I'd better say hello to the princess before I get started."

Abby replaced her mask, hauled up the dangling roll of insulation and went back to work.

After a few minutes with Lila, who seemed masterful at entertaining herself with angel drawings, Brady meandered through the house, checking and double-checking as he read through the calendar on his cell phone. He shot a group text to volunteers, then ordered the engineered hardwood flooring. He wrangled for a better deal but still winced at the final price increase.

"Sorry, Brady, it's the best I can do this year."

"Thanks anyway, Dale. Something's better than nothing." But he hung up discouraged. Getting material donations had been tougher this year. Tight economy. Rising prices. He was already dipping into his own account on this project, something he seldom had to do this early in the game. But Abby and Lila were worth it.

He headed back into the master bedroom, where Abby worked with her back to him. He stood in the doorway watching her. She was perfect for a guy like him. Brady's brain snagged on the word. Perfect height, he'd meant. She was slim with long legs and shapely arms that could reach high up on a wall to secure the batting. Her mink hair was pulled back in its usual ponytail and he wondered what she'd look like with all that dark hair falling around her shoulders.

She shoved a piece of batting against a two-by-six but quickly jerked her hand away, muttering, "Ouch."

"Splinter?" Brady pushed off the door and crossed the room.

She backed down the ladder, shaking her finger. "Got any tweezers?"

He arched an eyebrow. Seriously? Tweezers? Here?

"Let me see."

"I can get it."

"Don't be stubborn." He pulled her hand into his. Her fingers were long and slim but dwarfed in his big mitt. A sliver of pine was embedded beneath one of her nails. "That's a good one. Hold still, I think I can get it."

He moved into her personal space, a necessity under the circumstances, though one that made him more aware of her. As if he wasn't already struggling in that department. Warmth emanated from her, but her fingertips were cool. Feminine and soft.

Brady swallowed, forcing himself to concentrate on the splinter. He nabbed a protruding piece of wood and tugged. He felt her tense. "Sorry."

"Did you get it?" Big brown eyes lifted to his.

"Done." Quickly, he dropped her hand and took a step back. He didn't know what his problem was with this lady. "You okay?"

She shook her hand up and down. "Better, thanks. It'll be all right when it quits stinging. I thought you had to work on a paying job today. The Huckleberry Creek addition, right?"

"This is Thanksgiving weekend. Subconctractors don't want to work. I knocked off a few hours early."

"Won't your dad be upset that you're here instead of there?"

"Don't worry about my dad, okay?" Ever since she'd overheard his father's complaints about a nonpaying job, she'd been anxious.

"It bothers me when he gripes at you."

"I'm used to it." He forced a grin. "Arguing is our love language."

She started back up the ladder. "Seriously, Brady, why is he so hard on you?"

"Beats me. Conflicting personality types, I suppose." He'd always wondered why Dad picked at him but not the others. "He got worse after Quinn's injury."

He didn't know why he'd brought that up.

She paused on the third rung and turned toward him. "That's interesting. Do you know why?"

He had his suspicions. Dad had always favored Quinn, bragged about him in the coffee shops and ridden high on the wings of his son's success. After the accident, he was stuck with watching his second-best son play football. Brady never measured up to Quinn.

"Quinn was the smart one, the talented one. After he got hurt—" Brady frowned. "I don't know. This is a bad subject."

"He hurts your feelings, doesn't he?"

She was getting too close to the truth. Brady was the overgrown kid who had to work harder for his grades and to make the team. For Quinn, everything came easy. Quinn made Dad proud. Brady didn't. End of story.

Abby's dark eyes peered down at him. With a seriousness that clutched at his gut, she said, "No one is better than you, Brady. And no house is more important than your relationship with your father. Not mine or anyone's."

He heard what she didn't say, but for all their quarrels, Brady knew Dan loved him and was there for him. Abby had never known a father's love.

"Dad and I will be okay, Abby. He'll come around.

Don't worry about us." That was *his* job. He slapped the metal ladder, eager to change the subject. "Come on. Get busy, woman. Let's get this insulation installed so we can start the drywall. We've got a house to build!"

His statement brought a smile. Splinter forgotten, she gazed at him a moment longer before she took up the batting again and went to work. He watched her climb, admired her long legs and her work ethic, and then laughed at himself for the combined thought.

Toting a roll of batting to the opposite wall, Brady got busy, his mind humming with Abby Webster and a tangled version of "Jingle Bells."

Christmas makeovers were awesome. And this one might be the best of all. No use stressing over Dad today.

Every bone in Abby's body ached. She'd worked until after midnight last night and gotten up at dawn to start again. As accustomed to long hours and hard work as she was, construction challenged a new set of muscles. A new kind of fatigue.

But she would not complain. Not when Brady worked long hours, too, and tolerated his father's bad moods to give her and Lila this beautiful home.

"Time to close up shop," Brady said from behind her.

"Let me finish this one wall." They'd completed the first bedroom and moved on to another. She glanced at her watch. "I can't believe it's already this late."

Time had flown while they'd worked together, making small talk and banter. "We've accomplished a lot, but the princess needs to go home to bed."

"She's probably asleep on her play mat."

"She is. Or she was when I last checked." He walked across the space to her ladder. "The other princess needs rest, too. Come on down. You're tired. You barely stopped to wolf down that plate of leftovers I brought, and now your eyes are glazing over."

"But this wall—"

"Will be here tomorrow."

She brushed a weary hand over the top of her hair. "But I can't finish the job until after work. I'm at the diner tomorrow."

He frowned up at her. "What time?"

"Six."

Something hot flared behind his electric-blue eyes, a flash of lighting. "Why didn't you tell me that before? Get down from there now. You're going home."

If she hadn't been so tired, she'd have told him to take a flying leap. Instead, she accepted the command for what it was—concern—and climbed down. "I'll get Lila and head home."

"*I'll* get Lila. You go to the car."

Instead, she followed him into Lila's play space. Lila was fast asleep on her mat, a blanket tucked around her neck. "Did you cover her up?"

Brady frowned again. "Sure."

Something sweet and warm turned over beneath her rib cage. The man made her crush worse every day.

"Thank you." She carried Lila's walker but left her toys in the room for tomorrow.

Brady gently lifted Abby's daughter, taking care to keep the blanket snug around her. He nodded toward the exit. "Go ahead. I'll lock up after you leave."

Abby led the way to the car, opened the back door and stood aside for Brady to lower Lila into her car seat. He dwarfed the small car and had to duck low but completed the task like a pro. As her daughter snuggled deeper into the car seat without ever opening her eyes, Brady snapped her seat belt. Then, as Abby watched, he leaned in and kissed her baby on the forehead.

"Sweet dreams, princess," he whispered.

Everything inside Abby melted.

Brady maneuvered his big body out of the backseat and closed the door softly with a single shove of one giant hand. Lila didn't stir.

When Abby started around to the driver's side, he followed, opening the door for her. He was a well-mannered Texan, doing what a gentleman did. He couldn't realize how he was affecting her.

She stood in the open door with him on the opposite side. The dome light cast a straw-colored glow into the darkness though Brady's height hid his face in the shadows above the car.

"You did a great job today." His voice was deep and soft.

She crossed her arms against the chill and his charm. "So did you."

"If we weren't so busy—" he started to say but seemed to change his mind.

Her heart skipped a beat. "What?"

He glanced toward the house and then back to her. "It's cold. You should get home."

She hesitated a second before sliding into the driver's seat. "Good night, Brady, and thank you."

"See you tomorrow." He leaned in and touched her cheek. "Sweet dreams to you, too. You deserve them."

Thankfully, he slammed the door and stepped away before she could find her voice. Her chest ached with feelings she didn't want and couldn't afford to feel.

She lifted her hand and drove away. In her rearview mirror, he stood in the cold moonlight watching her leave. The giant man with the bigger heart.

"Oh, Brady."

Either she was very, very tired or her heart was in a world of trouble.

Chapter Nine

Brady didn't like to shop, but on this particularly cold Friday morning he'd been out and about on other business and walked past Wonder World, a local store with a little bit of everything. In the Christmas window display, a fold-and-play art studio complete with easel and neon-orange stool caught his eye. The little princess liked to draw and color. He'd been wondering what to get her for Christmas. Voilà. Problem solved.

Abby would say he shouldn't have, but she would relent. She was a soft touch with Lila.

He bought the item and had it gift wrapped by Mary Hill, the store owner who also happened to be Mayor Hanover's daughter.

"Is this for Amber?" she asked.

"No." He frowned. "You think Amber would like one, too?"

"Sure, she would. Little girls love to draw and paint."

Awesome. Two birds with one stone. He never knew what to get his little niece. Boys, like his nephew, were easy. Girls, a puzzle. Generally, he relied on one of his sisters. This, however, got him completely off the hook. Abby wouldn't be miffed because he'd also shopped for Amber. He loved it when a plan came together.

"Got another?"

Mary chuckled. "Want it wrapped, too?"

"Yes, ma'am."

As she worked, twirling ribbons and creating something beautiful with paper, she asked. "So who's the other lucky little girl? One of your Christmas projects?"

The question was asked in all kindness, but something about the term didn't sit right with Brady. Lila wasn't a project. Maybe she'd begun that way, but now…

"A friend's little girl," he said.

"Ooh, a friend." Mary, his mother's childhood friend and a woman he'd known all his life, raised her eyebrows. "Has someone captured the heart of one of Gabriel's Crossing's elusive Buchanon bachelors?"

He laughed and, without answering, took his packages and left. But her question swirled around inside his head the rest of the day.

He stopped at the appliance store and then the paint and lumber companies, making selections and gathering samples. Some were for Huckleberry Creek but most, he had to admit, were for Abby's house. He'd promised to let her choose and today was as good as any.

With his errands complete, he drove from project to project, making sure subs were in place and things were going smoothly. He did a bit of troubleshooting, rescheduled a couple of subs and wrangled with a vendor over delivery dates. Then he stopped by the Buchanon Built offices to check mail and work with Quinn on plans for a new construction job Dad had taken on. An addition to a local business.

Brady and Quinn were both miffed about the added work. They'd not planned for anything more until spring, when the current buildings would be finished. But, as always, Dad was the boss and expected Brady and the others to make the project happen. All the projects.

His father arrived, annoyed by a mistake made on the McGruder house.

"I thought you had that under control," he said to Brady.

"I spoke with Perry last week. He seemed to know the buyer wanted a heat pump instead of a furnace."

"Well, apparently he didn't know. And now we've got a furnace to pay for and replace."

Brady's heart sank. Delays and mistakes were costly in both time and money. Both issues irritated Dan more than anything other than the mysterious vandalism. "I'll get together with Perry and see what we can do."

"That house has to come in on time, Brady. It's already sold and the buyer is paying extra to move in before Christmas. Unless you get off your duff, your halfhearted attitude is going to jeopardize the deal."

Temper flared. Brady could feel his face and neck heating up like a long day in the Texas sun. "There's nothing halfhearted going on, Dad, but I can't be everywhere. You're killing us with your demands."

"My demands wouldn't be that hard if you'd keep your mind on business."

He stiffened. So that was where his father was heading. "I thought we had this resolved. You like Abby and Lila. You agreed they deserve a home makeover."

"Liking them has nothing to do with business. Fix the problem, Brady. I don't care what you have to do." Dan spun on his work boots and stalked off, slamming the outer door hard enough to rattle the metal building.

Brady ground his back teeth. He'd fix it. He always did.

At five, the other Buchanons closed the office and left. Quinn, on his way out, said, "Go home and forget this for a while, Brady. You're taking things too seriously."

"Easy for you to say. Dad's not on your back."

"All work and no play," Jaylee added with a flip of her long hair. "I have a date. You should try it sometime."

"Right. Like I have time for dates."

"I can think of someone who might be interested."

"No more setups with your friends. The last one approached stalker status."

Quinn clapped him on the shoulder. "I don't think she meant one of her friends, Brady. I think she meant one of yours."

He didn't have to ask who they meant.

With a grunt, he turned and went back to work.

He stayed at the office later than usual that evening, jockeying schedules and procuring the missing heat pump. The problem remained, though, that Perry couldn't return to install the unit for several days and another heat-and-air company wouldn't touch someone else's half-finished job. Unless he could figure out another scenario, the project was doomed to fall behind.

At seven, discouraged and rubbing the knot on his shoulder, he and Dawg knocked off for the day. He started home, changed his mind and drove across the railroad tracks to Cedar Corner. Abby's car was in the driveway.

"All work and no play." She was as bad as him.

He parked the truck and hopped out. The air had a sharp bite tonight, stinging when he sucked in air. The night was moonless, but a pale lemon light seeped from the sidelights of the red front door, a fancier entry than he usually put in his Christmas makeovers. In others he'd used a less expensive, utilitarian door, but this one had caught his eye and seemed right for Abby.

Dawg, eager to hang out with Lila, loped to the front porch and waited patiently, his tail thumping.

When they entered, Dawg sniffed the concrete before trotting down the hall toward Lila's playroom. Brady followed the sound of country music to find Abby in the future laundry room sweeping trash into a heap. The old radio he carried onto building sites pumped out Carrie

Underwood. Plumbing fixtures protruded from the walls, reminding him of the heat pump and the discussion with his dad.

Not happy thoughts. He turned his attention to the woman.

In hoodie, jeans and athletic shoes, with her hair in a ponytail, she looked about sixteen.

"How old are you?" he blurted without thinking.

"Twenty-eight." Her smile was quizzical. "That's a strange question. How old are you?"

"Thirty-three and feeling every minute of a hundred thirty-three." He held the dustpan while she swept the dirt onto the tray.

"Bad day?" She took the pan from him and leaned the broom in a corner.

Brady's past few hours rode his shoulders like a two-hundred-pound gorilla. "I'm tired, I'm hungry and I've had a lousy day. Let's go somewhere and cheer me up."

"What?" She blinked rapidly, puzzled and maybe a little amused.

He reached for her hand and tugged. "Come on. I'm serious. Forget about the house for one night."

"I—I'm at a standstill anyway. I don't know what else to do at this point. That's why I was sweeping."

"A few guys are scheduled to hang rock tomorrow night. Once the drywall is up, things go fast. There will be plenty to do." He tugged again. "Come on."

She gazed around the kitchen uncertain. "Well…"

"If it will make you feel productive, I have samples in the truck and we can pick out tile and paint colors over dinner and maybe watch some mindless TV."

He didn't know where the invitation came from. It was one of those spontaneous things, completely unplanned, but he wasn't backing down.

"TV? Where?"

"My house. We'll throw some steaks on the grill, nuke a couple of potatoes, toss a salad." The idea improved by the minute.

"Your house?"

"Is that a problem?"

"No... I—"

"I want you to see the cabinet stain I used. Golden oak. I think you'll like it in your kitchen, too." Actually, the stain was a last-minute thought to convince her, but he warmed to the idea of impressing her with his handi-work. He'd built that house from ground up, as far as he'd gotten, and he loved every rock and board.

"Well...I guess it would be okay. If you're sure you want to."

Nothing sounded better right now. "I'll get the prin-cess."

"I'll follow you in my car so you don't have to drive back here."

"Better ride with me."

"Why?"

"Do you know where I live?"

"No, but you can tell me. I follow directions well."

She did, indeed. As a helper on the project, she was a gem. He was, however, concerned that she'd get lost on the windy river roads. Lots of people did, but they had cell phones. Hers never seemed to be working.

"I'm on the outside of town, a little off the beaten track near the river."

"Oh." She seemed to be debating something.

"I'll bring you back here whenever you're ready."

"If you're sure it's not too much trouble."

He wished she'd stop staying that.

They drove over the railroad tracks and through town, down the T-shaped main street with satellite radio playing a mix of country's top forty and country Christmas. Overhead, long strings of multicolored Christmas bulbs cast rainbow reflections on the pavement.

"Pwetty, Mommy," Lila said from the backseat of Brady's SuperCrew cab. Next to her, Dawg sat like a human being with his nose pressed against the window.

Abby shifted in the passenger seat, caught Brady's smile in the dash-light glow and answered with one of her own. "Real pretty."

She didn't know what had come over Brady tonight and she'd almost refused his invitation. Being alone with him would be torturous given her crazy feelings though, admittedly, a pleasant kind of torture.

Years ago, she'd thought the same about Lila's father. Spending time with Warren and feeling loved had outweighed her good sense, though she'd learned soon enough that he was like everyone else in her life. His love was nothing but empty words with no depth, and when the going got tough, he was gone. No one kept her around for long.

Troubled by such morose thoughts when she had so much to be grateful for and the normally upbeat Brady had clearly suffered through a rotten day, Abby said, "What happened? Problems with your dad?"

"Partly." He turned down the radio volume and cut short a Blake Shelton song. "Today was one of those days when things went wrong and I let the pressure get to me."

They drove past the Buttered Biscuit. Except for the string of white icicle lights shining around the front window, the diner was dark and quiet, the norm in a town that closed up early even during the holidays.

"I think you handle pressure extremely well. I'm amazed at how you juggle construction sites, contractors, vendors, work on my house and all the other things you do that I don't even know about."

"Doesn't leave much time for a social life, as my siblings so kindly reminded me today."

Abby blinked. Social life? As in dating? "Was that why you invited me to dinner at your house? To get your siblings off your back?"

"What?" He glanced from the wheel to her, scowling. "No!"

"Then why, Brady?"

"Because I'm hungry and I don't want to eat alone. Because we have samples to look at. Because—" He shook his head. "Will you stop questioning my motives?"

Was that what she was doing? She'd been suspicious of others' motives from the time she was old enough to know everyone had an agenda and those agendas were primarily for their own benefit. If Brady was different, she'd be very surprised.

"I'm sorry. You've had a rough day and I'm making it worse. You can take me back to my car if you're sick of me already."

"Stop assuming I don't want to spend time with you."

She wanted to ask what he meant but bit her tongue, instead. She'd come along to cheer him up, not to aggravate him more. But the thought that he actually wanted to be with her made her feel suspicious rather than complimented. How pathetic was that?

She leaned back in the seat and looked out at the passing town, silent. Brady turned the radio up again.

At the stoplight, he took a left past the IGA and followed the winding road through a residential area that eventually opened into wooded countryside. After a few miles, when the pickup turned down a dark, empty country lane, Abby leaned forward to peer into the darkness.

"I can't see a house anywhere."

His teeth flashed. "You will."

Past a cove of leafless trees, bright security lights sud-

denly lit the darkness and shone on a large two-story structure with shadowy landscaped evergreens. From what she
could see, the house was built of river rock and timber
with wraparound balconies up top and a chimney reaching high into the darkness.

"Brady," she breathed. "This is beautiful."

"Better in daylight." But she heard pride in his voice.
"A work in progress. The lower level is basically complete.
The upper story, not so much."

"When do you have time to work on it?"

"Ah, here and there."

He pulled the truck to a stop and they went inside. Lila,
who had somehow managed to remain awake, said, "I like
your house, Bwady. And guess what?"

"What?"

"It's big like you."

Abby flushed in embarrassment. "Lila!"

Brady laughed. "It's big like me on purpose. And has
plenty of room for a certain little girl to wheel around."
He put her walker on the hardwood floor. "Go ahead. Explore. Dawg knows the way." To Abby, he said, "Want to
look around?"

"I do, but you're starved. I heard your stomach growling
on the way out here. Steaks on the grill first. Tour second."

He raised his palm in a high five. "You genius woman."

Companionably, they worked together in the gorgeous
golden wood and rock kitchen, both rustic and modern and
a testament to Brady's eye for detail and his building skill.

When the simple meal was ready, they gathered at the
table situated to the left of the granite-topped bar and near
a wall of windows that looked toward the river. Dawg
parked his behind on the polished hardwood next to Brady
and stared hopefully at the sizzling beef steaks.

Mealtime prayer had become a comforting routine, and
when Brady stretched his hands toward her and Lila, she

put hers in his and closed her eyes. Not surprisingly, his palm was hard and calloused. She liked the manly feel of his skin, a reminder that, regardless of her height and large bone structure, Brady was all male and she was female.

"Amen," Lila said at the end of a prayer Abby hadn't heard. She'd been too focused on the man, a fact that shamed her. She hoped God wouldn't hold that against her.

"Mommy, can we do this at our new house?"

"Do what, baby?" Abby unfolded her napkin and spread it in her lap.

"Hold hands and pway."

Brady turned a quizzical expression toward Abby.

"We never said grace at meals before," she said. "This is new to us."

"Prayer is ingrained in the Buchanons. A habit formed in childhood." He sliced into his steak with a knife and fork. "In my wilder days, prayer and church became rote and meaningless. Things I did to keep my parents off my case. Dumb on my part."

"You had wilder days?" Abby speared the steaming baked potato and swirled her fork in the butter-laced sour cream.

"Oh, yeah. Bad temper. Fights."

"Anyone who would fight with you has a death wish."

He laughed. "Another reason I had to get my temper and myself under control. I didn't want to hurt anyone. Football gave me an outlet for the aggression, but it took a relationship with God to really set me straight. Not that I'm perfect by a long shot. Just ask my family."

He was close enough to perfect for her. Maybe too perfect. She had started to trust him, depend on him and like him too much. She was falling for the big beautiful lug. Falling like a rock from the top of Mount Everest. The fall was exhilarating. The crash landing was going to kill her.

Chapter Ten

Brady was hyperaware of Abby tonight for reasons he didn't examine. She looked relaxed and pretty seated next to him on the leather sectional as they sorted through the tub of full-size tile samples. He liked seeing her smile and loved hearing her laugh, so he told wild stories about his childhood with six siblings. He'd brought other dates here once or twice but couldn't remember a time when an evening had been this enjoyable.

Quinn was right. All work and no play was taking a toll. Tonight he felt happier and more relaxed than he had in several weeks. Even Dad couldn't rattle him after that steak dinner and an hour or two alone with Abby in his favorite place.

At the opposite end of the sofa, Lila was propped like a princess on a stack of pillows with her hands behind her head, the stuffed toy he'd given her snuggled close and Dawg curled on the floor next to her, snout on paws. Lila had snuggled down with a blanket and Abby predicted she'd be asleep before the first cartoon ended.

He'd set her up on his Netflix account with a show Abby said she loved. A family of pigs frolicked across the screen, mindless TV as he'd promised Abby, though Lila was enchanted. Every once in a while, the little girl giggled and his heart squeezed. She was something special.

"It must have been crazy fun," Abby said in response to one of his tales.

"Completely nuts, as you can tell by Sunday afternoon. There was always something going on, someone to play with or harass—" he grinned, remembering "—as we boys often did to our sisters and each other. What about you? Any wild childhood antics?"

"You don't even want to know the answer to that."

"Sure I do. Come on. I've confessed that I terrorized my sisters on a regular basis. It can't be worse than that."

"I was in foster care, remember? Group homes can be crazy at times." Her smile was wry and a little sad. "Not always fun crazy, either."

He sobered. He'd forgotten that her childhood was vastly different from his own. She didn't talk much about herself but curiosity got the better of him. He wanted to know her. Not only her obvious struggles with money and medical care. Everything.

"What was that like, Abby? Growing up without parents. It had to be really difficult."

"Time has a way of softening the edges, but yes, it was hard having no family, no stable place to belong." She bent to the box at her feet and took out two tiles, examining each with care. "Special occasions were the worst."

No one to celebrate her birthday or attend school functions. No rowdy bunch in the stands to cheer her graduation.

"Do you remember any of your birth relatives?"

"Not really. I was told my grandmother turned me over to social services after my mother died when I was around Lila's age. Or as one social worker so kindly put it, she dumped me like a stray cat and never looked back."

Ouch. Brutal. "You weren't ever adopted?"

"Apparently, I wasn't the most appealing kid. Big feet, gangly, somber." She shrugged. "Not a sunny doll face like Lila. When I was thirteen a family *almost* adopted me, but things didn't work out."

Her casual acceptance of rejection twisted like a knife in the gut. Something that brutal had left scars, he was sure of it, though she covered them well. "What about your father?"

"He was never in the picture." She glanced toward her daughter. As she'd predicted, Lila's eyes were closed and her chest rose in rhythmic sleep, the pig family not enough to keep her awake. "He was a deadbeat dad who left my mother pregnant and disappeared. Like Lila's. I hate that I did the same thing to my own child. Someday she'll realize she has no dad and it will hurt her. I never meant for that to happen."

He'd wondered about the man she'd loved enough to have a child with. "What happened to him?"

She sighed, crossed her arms in that signal of discomfort she always used when she was uncertain. It made his chest ache to know that she was.

He scooted closer but didn't touch her—the temptation was strong, but he wasn't sure she wanted that from him.

"You don't have to tell me if it upsets you."

"I loved him, if that's what you're asking. He said he loved me, too, and I had visions of the family I'd always wanted and someone who would stay forever."

"But he didn't."

"Deep inside I knew it couldn't last. Nothing ever does. Still, when Warren couldn't deal with Lila's diagnosis, I was crushed. We fought for three days, but when he realized I was going to have this baby with or without him, he moved out. I haven't seen him since."

Warren. Somewhere out there was a complete jerk who called himself a man. A jerk who had walked away from his own sick baby. A jerk who'd broken Abby's already wounded heart and left her to deal with a frightening diagnosis all on her own. Alone, the way she'd always been.

Brady's temper flared. He clenched his fists, glad he didn't know where to find the creep. He was tempted to do some serious face pounding.

"His loss."

"Excuse me?"

"A beautiful woman like you. A sweet little princess like Lila. The man is an idiot." He tugged her arms apart and slid his hands down to hold hers. "You're somebody special, Abby. Don't let other people's failures convince you otherwise."

She shook her head, the dark ponytail swishing against the leather coach. Brody caught the tail in his fingers and rubbed the silk, again wishing to see her hair loose and long. Someday he'd slide the band from her hair and run his hands through the warm, heavy silk.

Someday.

"You've had a lot of letdowns in your life," he murmured, feeling tender and protective.

"Life is hard. It's the way things are."

"They don't have to be." When her soft espresso eyes snagged on his as if she longed to believe him, he couldn't resist saying, "Life is good, too. There are people who care about you." *People like me.*

They were close and he watched her black pupils dilate as he leaned nearer. He had the wild urge to kiss her and realized he'd wanted to kiss her for a long time. But beyond the obvious romantic feelings filling up his chest, he wanted to hold her and promise to be more than Warren or the dozen foster homes she'd drifted through in search of love and acceptance.

He trembled with the need to wipe away all her loss and hurt. He slid his arms around her and tugged her closer.

Her stiff body slowly melted into him. She fit as if she belonged there, not like some women who were so tiny he feared crushing them. Perfect.

Her soft breath warmed his ear and he might have brushed her hair with his lips.

She rested against him with a deep sigh as if she'd needed this. It occurred to him that no one had held Abby in a long time. She had no shoulder to lean on. No family to carry her through life's inevitable hard times. No one to hold her when she cried. No one to tend to her when she was sick.

He snugged her closer, kissed her hair again and made a vow. Abby needed him and he would be there for her. He'd be the one person in her life who wouldn't let her down.

Brady almost made her believe in the impossible.

Abby didn't know whether to run or grab hold and pray that the ride didn't end in disaster.

The next day at the diner, her thoughts were stuck on the evening with Brady as she slid plates of roast beef onto table six. The noon rush was on and the Buttered Biscuit was filled with businesspeople popping in for a hearty meal. The hot smell of grilled burgers mingled with the scent of fresh coffee and warm apple pie.

Every time the bell over the door jingled and cold air wafted inside, her heart leaped and she glanced up, hoping to see Brady.

Last night had touched her deeply. Snuggled in Brady's arms, they'd talked of heartaches and hard times, life and faith and each other.

She didn't want to fall in love with Brady. But she figured it was too late to turn back the tide. He was all the good things she'd ever dreamed of in a man.

And he scared her out of her mind.

When he'd driven her back to the car and followed her

home, she'd felt more protected than she'd ever felt in her life. She, a tall Amazon of a woman, didn't need protection, but knowing Brady cared enough to give it anyway fed a hungry spot in her soul.

He'd carried the sleeping Lila into his parents' home as if Abby hadn't done the task hundreds of time. She'd never had a partner in caring for Lila. She'd heard the adage that you don't miss what you've never had, but that wasn't true. Brady's kindness showed her what she and Lila were missing.

"Abby, order up!" Fran leaned through the server's window and looked at her with curiosity.

Aware she'd been in a fog thinking about Brady, she hurried to the window. "Sorry."

"Where is your head today, girl? Is Lila sick?"

"No, no. I'm sorry. Tired, I guess."

She should be tired but she wasn't. Not really. Brady Buchanon filled her head the way his big body filled a room. Completely.

He'd kissed her last night. Her. Awkward Abby from the wrong side of the tracks.

He'd been standing in the doorway to his parents' garage, the entry she used to access her rooms without disturbing the Buchanons. She'd switched on the light and followed him to the door, though she couldn't say why. The hour was later than either of them had planned, but their conversation had gone on and on until the Milky Way streaked the sky.

"Thank you for dinner," she had said. "And for everything."

"Thanks for cheering me up."

She scoffed softly, amused. "If my whining cheers you up, you're a sick puppy."

His mouth curved. "You never whine. That's part of

your charm. But you do cheer me up." He touched her cheek. "You."

While she absorbed the compliment like a thirsty camel, he leaned closer, his face serious, his eyes holding hers captive. "Good night, Abby."

"Good night." But she didn't step away from his touch, a touch that became a caress. The rough calluses of his manly hand stroked the softness of her face and sent pleasant chills through her.

Like a marble in a tin can, her heart rattled against her rib cage. When Brady leaned closer, mingling his breath with hers, the soft smile still on his perfect lips, her pulse went ballistic.

His mouth touched hers in a gentle, warm, heart-stopping kiss. Abby didn't notice or care about the late hour or the fatigue in her shoulders as time spun out through the garage and into the star-sprinkled night. Filled with a silken emotion, a gossamer thread of hope and pleasure she could ill afford to nurture, she kept her fists tight at her sides, afraid she'd throw herself against him and do something stupid.

When he stepped back, still holding her face with the tips of his strong fingers, his expression was serious. They stared into each other's eyes long enough for Abby to drown in his swimming-pool eyes before he dropped his hold. Then she watched him walk away, start his truck and drive into the darkness.

She'd awakened this morning wondering if it had all been a beautiful dream.

The bell over the diner door jingled and she looked up, aware that she was, once again, woolgathering instead of waiting tables.

Charla sailed past, balancing three dinner plates and slowing long enough to whisper, "It's not Brady. But you are so going to tell me what's going on with you two."

Heat rushed up Abby's cheeks. Thankfully, her skin was dark enough to cover her embarrassment.

"Charla," she hissed. "Hush. Nothing is going on."

But she couldn't keep her focus off the jingling bell and the diner doorway. For the rest of the day, she watched. Brady never came.

After work she drove to the building site. No one was there. The drywall team hadn't arrived and no progress had been made. With no work to do on the house, she and Lila ran some errands and headed to the Buchanon house for dinner.

Dan was in a dour mood at the table and even Lila's perkiness hadn't cheered the man, a rare turn of events for the charmer. When Karen asked what was wrong, he'd said, "Trouble on the McGruder site."

"Vandals?"

Dan braced his hands against the table and breathed out a harsh gust.

"We've gone more than a month without any trouble and now it has to happen on a nearly completed project with an incentive to finish early." He scowled at his dinner plate. "Sometimes I think someone knows exactly which properties are the most important to us. We had to pull a drywall crew from another job to repair the wall damage, a job that will also fall behind schedule."

So that explained Brady's absence and the missing drywall. Even though the reasons meant her house was behind schedule, she felt better. Brady wasn't avoiding her.

Karen passed Abby a bowl of green salad, her concerned focus on her husband. "What does Leroy say?"

"The police in this town are worthless, Karen. A year of trouble on Buchanon Built projects, and they don't have a clue."

"They're running shorthanded, honey. You know that.

Ever since Beau was in the car accident and Frankie moved to Dallas to get married."

Dan reached across the table to squeeze her hand. "You're right, as usual. What would I do without you?" He took a deep breath as if purposely calming himself and his hard face softened as he glanced at Abby. "This woman keeps my head on straight. I'm a fortunate man."

Karen patted his forearm. "You work hard. Problems like this are frustrating. But the stress will make you sick if you let it and I don't want you sick. I worry about you, Dan. You need to slow down."

Abby watched the exchange of affectionate concern with interest and a nearly constant longing in the pit of her stomach. A couple who had weathered many life storms, raised a large family and built a business still loved and needed each other.

Such relationships were possible. She knew they were. But were they possible for someone like her?

Two days passed and, though she drove to the home makeover each evening after work, no progress had been made and she'd barely spoken to Brady. She understood. Truly, she did. Brady was busy troubleshooting. The dry-wall crew was busy with repairs on the ransacked property. She didn't expect them to drop paying work to build her house. She also didn't want to impose on the Buchanons any longer than necessary.

She was stuck. She didn't want to ask the Buchanons about the delay and appear demanding, but she couldn't live on their charity forever. Brady didn't call or visit and she missed him.

"He's busy. Really busy," she told Lila, who wanted to know when Bwady was coming to see her.

The fact that she'd still not spoken to him since the night of the kiss activated a host of insecurities. Like schoolyard bullies, they bunched together to torment her. Maybe he regretted the impulsive, too-tired-to-think-straight action. Maybe he was glad for the extra work. Maybe he was avoiding her.

Common sense said none of that was true, but the bullies kept right on pounding away.

Gritty eyed from lack of sleep, Brady measured a sheet of gypsum for the McGruder repair. His drywall guys were working as fast as they could, but they weren't fast enough. Every experienced hand was needed. That meant him and any of the other Buchanons who could spare a minute. Subcontractors were exactly that. Subs. Though they were willing to work a little extra, Buchanon Built problems were not theirs to worry about. They went home to their families at six o'clock.

The Buchanons, on the other hand, had more to lose and pushed on. The whole family was exhausted, especially him and the twins who built trim for one job during the day and had replaced kicked-in cabinets and defaced trim here for the past two nights. The vandalism had escalated on this house and parts of the damage looked as if someone had taken an ax to the finish.

Escalated. He didn't like that word or the thought that whoever held a grudge against Buchanon Built might continue to go unchecked and do something worse.

He hadn't slept more than four hours a night this week and Dad was running about the same. They'd butted heads so many times today Brady refused to answer his father's calls. When he was tired, his temper was harder to control. He hated the failing and prayed about it plenty. The prayers must help because he wasn't in jail.

He paused to rub a hand over the back of his aching neck.

"Hey, Brady." Dawson stood in the doorway leading

into the kitchen, tool bag low on his hip and nail gun in one hand. "We're knocking off for the night. You should do the same."

"Not yet."

"Go home. Get some rest." Dawson's dimples were nowhere to be seen. His normally happy blue eyes were lined with fatigue.

"Go ahead. I'll lock up when I finish this last piece."

Dawson stepped into the garage and grabbed hold of the drywall sheet. "Let's do this, then. We both need sleep."

Grateful, Brady hoisted the board and led the way through the kitchen, where Sawyer was cleaning up. The leftie twin, powdery sawdust covering his clothes, looked as worn as his brother.

"We're going to knock this one out and head home," Dawson said as they passed, toting the drywall.

"Even Brady?"

"So he says."

Sawyer scooped a handful of nails into a box and followed his brothers. To Brady he said, "You're worried about finishing Abby's house?"

He was worried about way more than that where Abby was concerned. She must think he was as much a jerk as her ex. Not only had he kissed her and disappeared, he'd made promises he wasn't keeping. He wanted time to explore this thing with Abby, and he wanted her house finished. But every day he fell further behind on the project he loved most, a job that was joy, not work. Repairing the McGruder house, however, was hard, irritating, frustrating work.

"My focus is this site right now."

"Understood." Sawyer braced the plasterboard while Brady and Dawson nailed it in place. They'd had to cut out this entire wall, thanks to sheer destructiveness. "Christmas is only a few weeks away."

Brady scowled, a nervous knot in his belly. "Yeah."

"You're doing the best you can, Brady. Abby understands."

Did she? People had let her down all her life. He'd wanted to be the one who didn't, the hero she could lean on. He wanted to help her, make her life easier and better, and, yeah, he wanted to be with her. That one kiss had rocked his world, stirred him up worse than a blender.

He slammed the hammer one last time to set the nail head. "Got this, boys. See you tomorrow."

"You're going home, right?"

"Absolutely."

After his brothers drove away, Brady locked the doors, drove home long enough to shower, eat, feed his dog and collect his sleeping bag. He hadn't lied. He'd come home.

Then he and Dawg headed back to the McGruder house for the night.

Chapter Eleven

"Brady spent the night at the McGruder place again."

Abby overheard Karen and Dan talking as she entered the kitchen for a cup of morning coffee.

"He's doing what's necessary, Karen. It's his job as COO to make sure the job sites are safe, protected and on schedule."

Karen's usually serene expression darkened. "My son is human, too, Dan. You push him too hard."

"You think I push him too hard? I push everyone hard. Hard work is the way I've built a successful business, and someday the boys will appreciate my effort."

Karen handed her husband a cup of coffee, and, though she said nothing, her lips were tight.

Abby was considering slipping back down the hall when Karen spotted her. "Come on in, Abby. Don't mind us. We're all on edge these days."

"I wish there was something I could do." She was part of the reason they were behind, a fact that made her feel terrible.

Karen's expression relaxed into a smile. "Having you and Lila here cheers us up. Are you at the diner today?"

Abby poured herself a cup of coffee and shook her head. "My day off. I was hoping to work on the house but—"

She stopped, sorry she'd said a word. They had enough stress. "But the house can wait as long as you don't get tired of us in your way."

"No worry about that."

Dan went to the door and Karen followed, tiptoeing up for a murmur of conversation and a goodbye kiss. Abby turned away discreetly to give them a moment. As old as they were and even when they disagreed, the Buchanons still seemed in love. She could hardly fathom that kind of commitment.

After Dan left, Karen turned with a smile on her face. All trace of irritation was gone. "When you're finished with breakfast, would you mind running an errand for me? I'll keep an eye on Lila."

"I'd be happy to." Very happy. She felt like deadweight and jumped at any chance to be of help.

"Terrific. Brady will work all day without eating unless I force the issue. A man can't put in that much physical labor without fuel, so I'll fix him a hearty breakfast and you can run it over to him."

Abby's pulse did a stutter step. "Oh, okay."

Karen pulled a carton of eggs out of the fridge. "You sound unsure. Is there a problem with Brady?"

"No. Of course not. No problem at all." Unless she counted the little problem of her heart.

On the drive to the McGruder property, a gorgeous new residence Brady had proudly shown her a few weeks ago, Abby thought about what she would say and how she would behave when she saw him again. Should she give him a hug? Peck him on the cheek? Or pretend the tender moment in the garage that had sent her dreams spinning hadn't happened at all?

By the time she arrived at the job site, her hands shook and her belly jittered. She was a mess, behaving like a teenager. Wishing she'd brought Lila to break the ice, she took three deep breaths and carried the insulated bag of food into the house.

As she stepped inside, a chalky smell greeted her. White drop cloths covered the already carpeted and hardwood floors, and masking paper protected the windows and un-damaged wood. The custom showplace had almost been finished, and her stomach sickened to think of the time spent and the hard work that now had to be redone. Who-ever was damaging Buchanon Built properties had a se-rious ax to grind.

The house was silent but as she started down the hall in search of Brady, Dawg came out of the would-be den, stretching his long brindled legs.

"Hey boy, where's your master?" She rubbed his ears before looking into the den.

Brady, all six-and-a-half feet of him, lay sprawled in a sleeping bag, his eyes closed. She stood in the doorway and looked her fill. Even in sleep, fatigue lines edged his mouth and spoked around his eyes. A slight furrow wrinkled his brow. He was still the handsomest man she'd ever seen, but he was too exhausted to even hear her come inside.

And the front door had been unlocked.

Not wanting to startle him, she knelt at his side and set the fragrant insulated bag above his head. She longed to touch his face in the same gentle manner as he'd touched hers and to lean in and kiss him awake. She wondered how he'd react to such a bold action from awkward Abby the Amazon, as classmates had called her.

Before she could think too much, she placed her warm fingertips against his cheek. Overnight stubble made his skin scratchy in a good kind of way.

"Brady," she murmured.

Bright blue eyes flew open, full of confusion. He sat up abruptly, ready to battle any vandals who'd trespassed. When he realized it was her, his face changed and the look in his eyes softened. He seemed both happy and relieved that it was her.

"The front door was unlocked."

He stretched, shuddering. Heat pumped efficiently through the house but the plastic-covered floor was cool. "What time is it?"

"Eight."

"Man." He shoved aside the sleeping bag. "I let Dawg out earlier and afterward I lay down again for a minute." He made a sheepish grimace. "A minute turned into a couple of hours."

"Your mother said you're sleeping here every night."

"Got to. I can't take any chance of letting the vandals do any more damage. Although I kind of wish they'd show up again while I'm here, so I could nail them to the wall once and for all." His fists flexed as he gazed around the room. Brady Buchanon would be a formidable enemy. "This house must come in under schedule, and I have a week to make that happen."

"Can you do it?"

He sighed and scrubbed a hand over scratchy whiskers. "I hope so. I think so."

The vandalism wasn't his fault. He was a busy man, working as hard and fast as he could. Maybe too hard. His dad pushed him. Expectations were high all around. Everyone wanted a piece of Brady's time, including her. It was a wonder he didn't have an ulcer.

She set the insulated bag in front of him. "Eat. Your mom sent breakfast."

"I love that woman." He unzipped the bag. "Want some? I'll share."

She shook her head. "I've already eaten."

While he devoured the plate of sausage, eggs and toast, Dawg roamed in for a bite.

"Your kibble's in the garage," Brady said, but he tossed the dog a sausage patty anyway.

Abby sat cross-legged on the floor beside him. "So what's the plan for today?"

"Hopefully, the drywall crew will finish up here and move on to Huckleberry Creek." He crunched a bite of toast and chewed. "We haven't forgotten your house, Abby."

"You can't do everything. I understand that my house won't be finished anytime soon, certainly not by Christmas. I'm okay with that." She swallowed, hoping to sound convincing. "Really, I am. I never expected to have a new home in the first place."

"We'll get there." But she heard the doubt and concern in his voice.

"If the house is never finished, I'll get by. I always have." She hunched her shoulders inside the snug red jacket. Brady was under intense pressure and she was part of the reason. "There are some furnished apartments on Osage Street. I'll look at one today. The price sounded right and if I move there, I can get out of your parents' way. Then you won't feel so pressured."

Her budget would scream, but she'd saved money living with the Buchanons and she could add another day at the diner. Maybe two.

"You'll do no such thing." He pointed a fork at her, frowning. "You stay put. They want you there. So do I."

She wanted to believe him so badly. "You do?"

Did she sound as pitiful and needy as she feared?

Brady set aside his plate, dragged a napkin across his lips and scooted around to face her. "I hope you know the answer to that, Abby."

Her pulse started that craziness again, a wild hope thrumming through her bloodstream faster than flood water down the Red River.

He took her hand, stroking the tops of her fingers. "I

bulldozed your home, and I promised you a new one in its place. I'd be a sorry excuse for a builder and a lousy friend to leave you stranded. I plan to bring this project in on time no matter what I have to do."

Abby's raging heart slowly descended back to earth. It was all about the Christmas makeover for Brady. It wasn't about the pair of them or the sweet kiss they'd shared, a kiss she'd read more into than he'd intended. It wasn't about the fact that she was in love with him. Brady's focus was her house and his Christmas project, not her. She was only Abby, the foster kid, the charity case.

Abby was acting strange.

Brady had noticed the way she'd gone quiet before hurrying away as soon as he'd finished breakfast. The drywall crew had arrived as she'd left so he'd had no more opportunity to question her. He would, though—if he ever found an extra minute.

"Hey, Brady." Dell, the best drywall man in this part of Texas, came into the kitchen where Brady was putting hardware on the cabinet doors. "We'll be out of here by noon if you want to call in the painters."

"Thanks, Dell. You're a lifesaver." The screwdriver whirred as he finished a knob. "I can't tell you how much I appreciate the effort your crew put in on this."

"Christmas is coming and Buchanon paychecks always cash."

They both laughed. He knew what Dell was saying. "Yeah, but you went above and beyond this time around."

"You, too." Dell scratched a patch of drywall mud on his arm. "Sorry about that waitress's house. Are she and her little girl going to be okay until we can get there?"

"They're okay." He'd see to it. "Abby's not a complainer."

She'd touched him with her offer to move into one of the awful apartments on Osage. Touched and scared him.

He wanted to keep her close. She and Lila both needed and deserved the Buchanon family Christmas experience. They would love it. And he wanted her there, too. Abby was special, like her daughter, but in a different way. He hadn't liked a woman as much in a long time.

Dell disappeared and Brady took out his cell to inform the painters. He knew a couple of guys willing to add some extra hours. Christmastime was good for that. Everyone needed a little extra money for the holidays.

He'd no more than hung up when his phone vibrated and an unfamiliar number flashed on caller ID. Relieved not to see his father's name, he answered.

When the call ended, he was in a daze. Slowly, he slid the smartphone into his pocket and looked heavenward. "Thank you."

This call truly was the answer to his prayers.

Later that afternoon, Dawson sauntered into the Mc-Gruder house carrying a bag that smelled suspiciously like burgers. Brady glanced at his watch. A long time had passed since his sweet wake-up breakfast with Abby.

Dawg suddenly appeared from nowhere and raised his nose in the air.

"You look…better," Dawson said, shoving the bag against Brady's happy-dancing belly. "What happened? Santa Claus come early?"

"I think he may have."

Dawson's dimple flashed. "Been sniffing too much sawdust, brother? Burgers aren't that big of a deal."

Brady laughed, his mood significantly elevated. "The burger counts, but no, that's not the reason. Wait till I tell you the news."

"Talk while I work. I want this trim up and finished today."

"You and me both, bro." He extracted the burger, paper

crinkling and took a giant bite. The burst of dill pickles and mustard stung his taste buds in a good way. He tossed a French fry toward Dawg. The mutt caught it in midair and dispatched the potato in one gulp.

Dawson strapped on his tool belt and sauntered out to the garage, where sawhorses were set up next to the table saw. Brady followed, eager to share his news with someone.

A pile of trim lined one wall. Dawson took up a board and began to measure. The tape made a high-pitched whir and snapped shut before he hung it back on his tool belt.

As he aligned the trim on the saw guides, the dimpled twin glanced at Brady through safety goggles. "So what's up?"

"TV Ten wants to do a feel-good Christmas piece on Abby's home makeover."

"Nice. Dad will be happy. He loves free publicity."

"A TV spot might get him off my case for a while."

"Can't be a bad thing."

Dawson activated the saw and Brady chewed while the machine screeched. The burger was nearly gone. He'd been hungrier than he'd realized.

"I don't think you get it, Dawson," he said. "This program is more than getting Dad off my case. Not that I wouldn't love that little gift in my Christmas stocking."

Dawson hefted the trim and blew off the sawdust. "What, then?"

"I'm behind on Abby's house."

"I know that. We're behind on everything."

"I'm over budget, too, and Dad is not friendly with the purse strings this year."

"So?"

"If worded correctly, the TV spot could bring in donors, volunteers, people who are looking to do something good for someone else at Christmas while getting a little promo for themselves."

Dawson headed back into the house with Brady trailing behind. He stuffed the rest of the burger in his face and grabbed his nail gun from the counter as he passed.

His brother aligned the mitered corners, holding the trim in place while Brady shot in the nails.

"What did Abby say about being on television?" Dawson asked. "She's a quiet person. Proud, too, remember?"

Brady frowned. He remembered, but this was different. If the TV feature went as he hoped, she'd be the big winner. And he wouldn't have to worry about her crazy idea of moving out of his parents' house before Christmas.

"I haven't told her yet, but she'll be thrilled. I'm sure of it."

Abby was not thrilled. She was mortified.

Her heart sank and her face heated as Brady told her with much enthusiasm that the local television station wanted to film a Christmas feature about her, Lila, and the Buchanon Built Home Makeover.

"The public clamors for this kind of story, especially at Christmas," Brady was saying as they walked through her unfinished house with Lila alongside in her walker and Dawg trailing behind. "According to the reporter— Marvella Mayes—a feature at this time of year will generate the kind of positive publicity that brings volunteers and donors out of the woodwork. If we want to finish the house sooner rather than later, we'll need all the help we can get."

Abby recognized the name. Marvella Mayes was a sharp African-American reporter with a genuine way about her who specialized in tear-jerker stories. Normally, Abby wouldn't miss one of the reporter's features, but she cringed at the idea of *being* one of the features.

"Would I have to be on TV or can you do it all?"

"Me? Why would they want my ugly mug when they

can have this." Brady scooped Lila into his arms. "Look at this face." He gently squeezed her daughter's cheeks between his thumb and pinky until her lips pooched out. "Who wouldn't love a face like that?"

Lila scrunched up her nose, crossed her eyes and stuck out her tongue. Brady tickled her under the chin and Lila wiggled against him, giggling madly.

"A star in the making," Brady declared, and Lila giggled harder. "Hollywood, here we come."

"Over my dead body." But Abby couldn't help smiling at the exchange. "Really, Brady, I think you should do the interview. I'd be awful in front of a camera. I don't even like to have my picture taken. You're a natural with people."

"You and the princess will slay the dragon and win hearts all over Texoma. It's a win-win deal."

She couldn't quite see the win-win he obviously visualized. She hated the idea. Hated being the object of pity. Her stomach churned with painful memories of being exactly that too many times.

Abby gnawed the inside of her cheek, battling the sense of obligation to the Buchanons, especially to Brady, against her need to stand on her own two feet.

Brady seemed convinced this was the way to go and the thing to do. She didn't want to disappoint him. After all, in the end, she and Lila would have a beautiful new home because of his generosity.

Given the stress he was under, refusing ranked right up there with spitting in his face. Accepting meant the real possibility of public humiliation.

Abby breathed in the smell of new wood. All around lay the unfinished brainchild and handiwork of a man with good intentions. Now, his good intentions weren't enough. He needed help.

Screwing up her courage and swallowing a boatload of screaming, crying anxiety, she made a decision. If a TV spot would help Brady and the Buchanons, she owed it to them to at least try.

"I'll be awful."

Brady eased Lila back to her walker and slung a friendly arm around Abby's neck, pulling her against his side. "You'll do it?"

"If you promise to do most of the talking."

"Deal!" He kissed her on the forehead with a loud smack. "This interview is the answer to our prayers, Abby, and we'll have a blast. You won't regret this."

She already did.

Chapter Twelve

The morning of the scheduled interview Abby's stomach threatened revolt. She skipped breakfast and started getting ready hours before the taping.

When the tape aired tomorrow night at six and ten, everyone at the diner would be watching. Given Brady's enthusiastic promotion, the whole town and all of Texoma land could very well watch Abby Webster make a fool of herself.

"It's important to Brady," she whispered to the bathroom mirror. Her face was pale and she thought she might throw up. She couldn't imagine how much worse the actual interview would be. "Help me, Jesus."

The words came unexpectedly. She stared back at her surprised and puzzled eyes. She'd been going to church, praying with the Buchanons, but those things had been for them. Little by little, she must have absorbed their faith, because today she wanted the prayer to be real for her, from an anxious heart to God above.

She closed her eyes as hot tears pushed at the backs of her eyelids. Not tears of fear or embarrassment but of a tender tugging deep in her spirit.

Scared and nervous and feeling terribly alone, she whispered, "I've never known You before, Jesus, but I want to."

You'll never be alone again. The thought came out of nowhere and she knew it wasn't hers.

The room suddenly seemed brighter and her unruly insides settled. If that was Jesus, she wanted Him around all the time.

This interview wasn't about her. The ultimate purpose was to give Lila a healthier, more accessible home. She wanted that with all her heart. The interview also promised a means of giving back to the generous people who'd made the dream house possible. A short television interview was the least she could do.

"I can do this," she said, though her voice shook again at the thought of cameras.

She dressed Lila in an outfit she'd intended for Christmas, a fluffy red dress with ruffles and a white sash that looked amazing with Lila's dark brown hair and eyes. She combed and curled the wavy hair, and finished it off with a red side bow, smiling proudly as Lila toddled off with her walker to show her finery to Karen and Dan. Her baby was beautiful.

At the reporter's request, Abby wore jeans and a sweatshirt to appear as if she was working on the house. Which she would be. Considering her limited wardrobe, she was relieved, but she'd pressed a crease into the faded jeans and scrubbed her tennis shoes with an old toothbrush. She'd do her best not to look like a poverty-stricken, homeless bum even if she was one.

As she debated between leaving her hair down and her usual ponytail, a knock sounded at the door. Her heart leaped into her throat and nearly choked her.

"Just breathe. God is with you," she murmured to the mirror, borrowing the words Karen had spoken earlier. This time she knew they were true.

To the door, she called, "One minute." Sleeking her

twice-washed hair into a tail, she secured it with an elastic band and hurried to the door. Brady stood in the hallway.

"Ready?"

Panic stung through her veins. So much for her calm. "Is it time?"

"Just about. The princess looks like a…princess." He beamed his thousand-watt smile. "And you, you're perfect. The two of you are going to be awesome."

She blew out a nervous breath. *God is with me. I'm not alone.* And followed Brady to his truck.

The next night Brady gathered with the entire Buchanon clan around the television at his parents' house to watch the interview. Abby tried to beg off, but Brady had snagged her hand and dragged her into the living room. She'd been extremely nervous during the interview, and if he'd known how white her face would get and that her hands would tremble, he'd never have asked her to do it. But she had, and admiration had filled his chest for the way she'd persevered. Even better and sweeter, she'd turned the focus on him and Buchanon Built, grasping every opportunity to make them look good.

Abby was something special.

A couple of times during the taping she'd floundered, but he'd stepped in to explain his passion for Christmas and the home-makeover process, the remaining work to be done and the need for volunteers. Marvella, as she'd promised, plugged Buchanon Built and opened the door for donations and experienced workers. He prayed they would be successful.

"Come on now," he said to Abby. "You don't want to miss Lila's debut. She charmed the socks off that camera crew."

It was true. Lila, in her walker and fluffy red dress, became the focus of the feature. With childlike poise and delight at being the center of attention, she'd pulled her walker through the unfinished house, describing every detail she could remember. Especially the details about the princess room Bwady was building for her.

Brady couldn't have been more pleased with the results. This was going to work. He was certain of it.

As they gathered, the clan helped themselves to bowls of steaming beef stew and thick slices of corn bread before settling in front of the television. Abby, he noticed, didn't eat a thing.

When the news came on, Abby grimaced and huddled inside her crossed arms. Lila, seated on Dan's lap, pointed at the TV and said, "There's that nice lady."

When a close-up shot of Lila came into view, tongue between her teeth as she concentrated on moving the walker, the little girl squealed and clapped. "It's me. It's me. Guess what, Mommy? I'm in the TV."

Abby's smile was wan. "Shh. Let's listen."

"I'm recording." Dan winked at Lila. "She'll be able to watch it all she wants. I'll make a DVD for you to keep."

Under her breath, barely loud enough for Brady to hear, Abby said, "Oh, great. Eternal evidence."

Brady chuckled and hooked a finger on to the pinky pressed to her side. It was ice-cold.

A hush fell over the room as the interview continued. Brady glanced at his father and was pleased to see him nodding, a gleam in his eyes. For once, maybe his father approved of something he'd done.

Abby was more nervous now than she'd been this morning, and she'd nearly fainted then. Suddenly, her oversize face appeared on the screen. She covered her eyes, but her voice went right on speaking in a Texas twang that couldn't be hers. Did she really sound like that?

She peeked through her fingers and, sure enough, it was

her, although her normally tan face was pale and she had licked her lips too often. They'd been as dry as her throat.

The shot moved to Brady, who explained about the project and his love of Christmas. That part she enjoyed. His good looks could sell ice in Antarctica.

He paraphrased a Bible verse. "'To whom much is given, much is required.' Our family and business has been blessed so we want to give back to our community. What better way to show Christ's love during the holidays than to give someone a new home, especially someone as deserving as Abby and her daughter?"

The interviewer turned to her. She hated this part. Hated it. She'd even prayed this section would be edited out.

"Abby," Marvella said, "I understand you grew up in foster care. Can you tell us a little about that and how your difficult childhood affects your desire to be the recipient of Brady's Christmas project?"

Abby cringed as the interview continued. She'd swallowed her pride and the nasty taste in the back of her throat to answer, but she couldn't quite get past feeling diminished. She was nothing. A project.

When the feature ended, a jubilant Buchanon clan talked at once, high fives all around.

"Great job, Brady." Dan said. "Brilliant the way you worked in the reward for information on the vandalism."

"Maybe we'll get some takers."

Abby focused on Brady's wide grin. She'd done the interview for him and he was happy. Good enough. Her embarrassment would pass. It always had—though every episode left a small, throbbing scar.

The next week was crazy. By Monday morning Brady juggled a glut of volunteers and donations for Abby's house with his usual overload of work. Relieved more than he'd thought possible not to let Abby down, especially after he'd convinced her to submit to the interview, he'd purchased Dawg two extra sausage patties at the diner while he'd gone over the list of offers with an overwhelmed Abby.

The appliance store donated top-of-the-line kitchen appliances in exchange for the publicity Brady had promised for those who stepped up to the plate. The furniture store offered Abby a gift certificate to choose a living room suite. An individual donated princess furniture, and the latest and best accessibility tools for Lila. Lumber and hardware stores vied with each other to give fixtures, flooring, paint and supplies.

By Friday, Brady's Christmas spirit returned in force even though he was snowed under. It was a good kind of busy as he coordinated work at the makeover—now charging full speed ahead—and directed the Buchanon Built projects. The McGruder house came in on time, a major accomplishment that he credited to diligence and plenty of prayer. He could finally sleep in his own bed, knowing the owner had taken possession. Best of all, Mom told him that Abby, in her quiet, private way, had committed her life to the Lord.

Friday afternoon he popped into the Buttered Biscuit for a late lunch and a little time with Abby. A man had to eat and he liked company. Hers. So he timed his meal to coincide with her afternoon break.

With the noon rush over, she was sweeping the floor while Charla and Jan polished tables and replenished condiments. Stenciled snowflakes decorated the front windows and a miniature tree blinked beside the cash register. Two pie eaters sat at the counter below dangling ornaments while the Spencer sisters shared a table next to the door, a pile of shopping bags and wrapped gifts at their feet. Brady lifted a hand in greeting—he'd dated Shannon for a time—though his attention was riveted on a dark-haired waitress with a shy smile and a red Santa hat.

The swoopy feeling he attributed only to Abby stole his breath.

"Break time, Abby." Jan leaned over an empty table, scrubbing away. Her necklace of tiny Christmas lights blinked a rainbow against the damp table. "Grab some lunch while you can."

Abby glanced around the half-empty room, then parked the broom in the corner and came in his direction.

"I like your hat." He touched the jingle bell on top with his index finger and they both grinned at the tinny tinkle.

"Jan's big on celebrating the season."

The other employees wore them, too. "I'm good with that. The bigger the better."

"I noticed." Her smile widened. "What would you like for lunch?"

"Whatever's ready."

"Today's special. Meat loaf and mashed potatoes."

"Perfect."

"Jan baked cherry pie this morning."

"I knew today was going to be a good one."

She whisked away, returning in minutes with his food and a plate for herself. While they ate he filled her in on the latest progress on the house.

"The plumbers are there to set the new fixtures."

"I can't believe how fast things have gone this week."

"Many hands make light work. But trust me, we have plenty left to do."

"I have errands to run after work but as soon as I can, I'll be there to do my part."

"No one could ever call you a slacker."

She beamed as if he'd paid her the world's best compliment. "You either, Mr. Buchanon. I think you border on workaholic."

The comment set him back. Him? Like his dad? No way.

He chewed the homey meat loaf, considering. This year

had been exceptional. He didn't always maintain this kind of manic schedule. Did he? But then, didn't his siblings regularly tease him with the all-work-and-no-play joke?

"Your house isn't work. It's fun. Christmas projects are what I do for a hobby."

"Looks like work to me. What do you actually do to relax?"

He laughed and leaned back in his chair to study the queen of workaholic. "I could ask you the same. When did you last do something for fun?"

"I—" She opened her mouth, closed it, opened it again. "Lila and I came to your house for steaks and watched TV."

"That was too long ago. We should do it again." And again and again. "Tomorrow night is the Christmas parade and chocolate festival. Let's do it. You and me and Lila."

Yeah. He hadn't come in here to ask her out, but why not? He'd been wanting to spend time with her that had nothing to do with her house, and he never missed Gabriel's Crossing Christmas events, especially the parade.

"I was already planning to go. Lila's riding on the church float."

He knew that. The little princess had nearly levitated with excitement at participating in the Christmas parade.

An awful thought struck him in the gut. Like a sledgehammer.

"Are you going with someone else?" And if she was, who was the creep and why hadn't he known she was seeing another guy?

"No. I'd thought about asking Charla but she already has plans."

Hurray for Charla.

"We'll go together. Me and you. Afterward, we'll grab the princess and head to the chocolate festival." He aimed a forkful of cherry pie at her. "What do you say?"

Soft espresso-colored eyes gazed at him as if he must

have an ulterior motive. He did. Her. Did he have to spell it out for her? Me Tarzan. You Jane. Let's go to the parade together.

"Okay."

Brady blinked. Twice. Had she said yes without an argument? Without an explanation?

"Sweet."

Life kept getting better and better.

He popped a bite of cherry pie into his mouth. Sweet, indeed.

Abby parked her Honda in the lot outside Lila's day care. The car needed an oil change and she added that to her to-do list, stressing about the cost in light of the fast-approaching holiday. The new battery had set her back a little.

She'd put some toys and clothes on layaway for her daughter, but she desperately wanted to give gifts to the hospitable Buchanons as well as put money in the offering plate at church. God was being so good to her. She needed to give back.

Being a new Christian at Christmas was pretty special. She felt a new appreciation and kinship to the holiday that had been missing before. Funny how easily the change had come, as if her spirit had been waiting all this time for her to acknowledge the need for Christ.

This newfound relationship was something else she owed to the Buchanons. Her IOU list was growing longer by the day. They were good people. Giving to others was as much a part of them as the construction business. They'd never intentionally make her feel obligated but, of course, she did.

Exiting the car, she pulled her puffy red jacket closer against the north wind and started across the gravel parking lot. Cold stung her ears and nose. Her eyes watered.

She hoped the arctic front moved on through before to-morrow night's parade.

She was still shocked that Brady had asked her to go with him. Not as his latest charitable act but as a date. A real date.

She'd been in a great mood all the rest of the day. When she'd told Charla, her friend had said, "Girl, Brady Buchanon has had his pretty blue eyes on you for a long time. You better grab that man. He's a keeper."

Grab him. As if she could.

She stepped inside Huckleberry Play School, where she was greeted by children's voices and activities. Brightly colored Mother Goose murals filled the walls along with child-made Christmas crafts and ornaments. Lila had brought home a star made of glued craft sticks and silver glitter to add to the Buchanon tree.

Christina came out of her office. "Hi, Abby. Could we talk a minute before you pick up Lila?"

"Sure." Curious, she followed the owner inside the office. She'd paid her bill, hadn't she?

"Have a seat," Christina said as she settled behind a cluttered desk and folded her hands on top. "Lila had another accident today."

"Oh." Abby's hand flew to her lips. "Why didn't you call me?"

"We took care of her with the extra clothes in her locker, but, Abby, this is the second time this week. The fourth time this month. The teachers are maintaining her schedule, but it's not working."

"I'm so sorry. I—"

"I'm sorry, too. Really sorry. Lila is a wonderful little girl and we adore her, but if I make an exception to the rules for her, I'll have to do the same for everyone. This is a play school for toilet-trained children. Parents expect that. So do my employees."

"Have there been complaints?"

"Yes." Christina sucked in a deep breath. "Please understand that I'm in a bad position here and feel I have no other choice but to ask you to find another day care for Lila."

Abby's happy bubble burst. Another day care she could trust with her child? At a price she could afford that could accommodate her long hours? Where? She pressed her lips together, stung and worried.

Christina leaned forward, her kind face full of compassion and regret. Abby didn't blame the day-care owner. She'd known the rules when she had enrolled her daughter, and Christina had looked the other way more than once.

"You're paid up until Christmas. After that…"

Abby nodded and rose, her back stiff. "I understand."

Stomach heavy as if she'd swallowed a brick, she collected Lila and started to leave. Christina followed her to the door. "I'm really sorry, Abby."

Abby didn't answer. She couldn't with the tears burning at the back of her throat. Rejection of herself she could deal with. Rejection for her sweet, sunny, innocent daughter ripped her apart.

Sorry didn't begin to cover it.

Chapter Thirteen

"Everything all right?" Brady took Abby's gloved hand as they walked back to First Street from the church parking lot where the children riding the float had gathered. Charity, who taught Sunday school and was riding with the children, had taken charge of a very excited Lila.

"I'm fine. Why?"

"Just a feeling I have." Abby was always quiet but since he'd picked her and Lila up at the family home, she'd barely said a dozen words. Was it something he'd said or done? Had she come with him out of a sense of obligation and now regretted the decision? "You were deep in thought last night, too, but I figured you were concentrating on the house."

"I was." Her boot heels made tapping sounds on the sidewalk. He fit his steps to hers, pleased at how well they fit. Did she notice it, too? "I'm still in awe of all that's been done."

Okay. He could accept that. Her mind was on the makeover. Still, she didn't seem as animated as he'd expected and he couldn't shake the feeling that she was upset.

"Construction is going well. I'm hopeful—" He stopped there, not wanting to promise something he couldn't deliver. "Colder tonight than I'd expected."

Perfect for snuggling. He didn't say that, either. He was content with her close to his side and her hand in his.

"Last year we were too hot."

"The guys in Santa suits nearly melted." He chuckled. "Christmas weather in Texas is unpredictable."

The tall, hovering streetlights illuminated the chilly night in long, finger-shaped shadows of silver. Residential homes added a glow with their Christmas lights and yard art, including a bell-ringing inflatable Santa and a waving Frosty. Down the street, the high school marching band warmed up with "Deck the Halls."

Other couples walked toward the parade route and snatches of conversation danced on the crisp air. Brady's breath puffed vapor as he considered the woman at his side. She reminded him of his sister's cat, soft and quiet but mysterious. Abby kept her feelings close to the vest. Buchanons weren't very good at that.

"Want some hot chocolate?" he asked when they passed an open coffee shop. "Or popcorn? The cheerleaders have a popper set up next to the courthouse."

"I smell it," she said, and lifted her nose to the fragrant air. "Maybe after the parade."

Brady chose the tall courthouse steps as their spot to watch the event. A crowd had already gathered, including friends and business acquaintances and any number of people who frequented the diner. Brady figured he knew practically everyone in Gabriel's Crossing, at least by name. Events such as this were perfect opportunities to say hello.

From the south end of First Street, a police siren wailed to announce the parade's beginning. Police Chief Leroy in his shined-up cruiser crept by and waved. Behind him came the ambulance and fire trucks with Sparky the fire dog riding up top, a bandanna around his neck. Abby made a cute squeak of excitement. Brady gazed down at her with a smile. Her cheeks glowed and her brown eyes danced. Whatever had been bothering her was washed away in the simple pleasure of a hometown Christmas parade. Good. He wanted her to enjoy tonight.

The emergency vehicles wailed on past and Abby laughingly covered her ears. Teasing, Brady added his giant paws to the sides of her head and they both laughed as he dwarfed her.

Behind the sirens marched the American Legion Color Guard and the high school band, followed by a dozen floats decorated in simple poster-board and crepe-paper designs and lit by Christmas strands attached to the sides of flatbed trailers. Some participants sang carols. Others waved or tossed candy into the crowd. Children scurried for the peppermint and Tootsie Roll treats.

Christmas spirit was tangible and Brady felt it to the tips of his very cold toes.

"There she is." Abby bounced up and down, pointing. "Look, Brady. She's coming."

Brady had watched Gabriel's Crossing parades his entire life and participated in many. This year an employee drove a Buchanon company truck and the employees' kids, dressed as elves, tossed mini Buchanon Built Frisbees into the crowd. He'd always enjoyed this event to kick off the countdown to Christmas, but this year was even better as he watched Abby watch Lila.

The love she showed for her little girl moved him. He could fall for a woman like her, a woman who shared his passion for family.

Taking her by the shoulders, Brady maneuvered them closer to the street to be sure Lila could spot them. Standing taller than most, he figured she'd notice him first.

"Bwady! Mommy!"

Lila's gold tinsel halo wobbled above her head and glistened in the reflection of the white lights dancing around the float. Dressed in a white angel costume, her dark hair curled around her shoulders and her cheeks pink with joy above a glowing smile, she fit the part. She perched in her wheelchair at the head of the nativity scene, waving her tiny hand at everyone. Other church children filled the parts of the Holy family. Behind them, a small choir sang "Silent Night."

The sweet scene reminded him of all that was good about Christmas, about the ultimate gift God had given to the world. It reminded him, too, that he cared deeply for the little angel on the float. Her biological father was a fool for tossing her aside. He never wanted Lila hurt by that abandonment, but she would be and there was nothing he could do to stop it.

"She's gorgeous," he murmured against Abby's hair.

Abby raised shining eyes to his and he couldn't help saying, "So are you."

Abby's full, beautiful mouth fell open in what he hoped was pleasant surprise. They were in a crowd in the middle of a parade, but Brady dipped his head and touched her lips with his. Her breath was warm; her lips were cold.

"You need warming up," he murmured, and pulled her closer.

Abby didn't object. In fact, when he slid his arm around her waist, she returned the favor.

Side by side, snuggled close against the cold, they watched her daughter, the child he'd come to love ferociously, slowly move on down the street. The church float was replaced by a marching Boy Scout troop and then the local dance school in red-and-white fur, tap-dancing to a boom-box version of "Santa Claus Is Coming to Town."

Abby shivered and Brady moved to cradle her inside his coat and block the wind. He felt cozy and comfortable, as if he and Abby belonged together this way.

When the parade ended with a very jolly Saint Nick

*ho-ho-ho*ing from a horse-drawn sleigh, Abby turned in his arms, smiling. "That was wonderful."

"Best ever," he said, close enough to consider kissing her again, but he refrained. He rocked her back and forth, grinning into her happy face. The crowd began to disperse, but he wanted to stay right here with Abby in his arms and not a care in the world. No business pressing. No calls from Dad. Nothing and no one but him and Abby enjoying each other in the spirit of Christmas.

He could get used to this.

Abby put a hand to his chest. "We have to go get Lila."

She was right. They did. With a regretful sigh, Brady led the way down the street. "Chocolate Festival?"

"Oh, yeah."

He laughed. "I thought so. Hot chocolate and all the goodies."

They collected the overexcited four-year-old from the church parking lot, placing her in the wheelchair for easier travel along the streets. Stores stayed open late on parade night and Brady wheeled Lila close to window displays. Unlike his niece and nephew, who wanted everything under the sun for Christmas, Lila asked for nothing, not even the kitchen play set that made her say, "Ooh, Mommy, look." She broke his heart.

"How about that hot chocolate?" Abby said in what was an obvious attempt to distract Lila from the expensive toy.

"Hot chocolate coming up. Hang on tight." He performed a wheelie with the chair and set off down the street, earning a giggle that tickled his chest. But even as the conversation turned to chocolate, Brady didn't forget about the kitchen play set.

"I've never seen this much chocolate in my life."

The community center had been transformed into the most delicious-smelling place on earth. Abby stared around the huge hall at tables and tables of treats, all of them following the chocolate theme in some way. Gift baskets, candy treats, cakes, pies, boxes of dipped fruits and nuts were for sale along with individual bite-size offerings. She never attended this event. The goodies were not only too tempting but an unnecessary expense.

"Indulge. I have a running tab with the head chocolate guru."

She bumped his side. "Silly."

"Serious. Check it out." He nudged his chin toward the cash register and a robust blonde woman in a red-and-white-striped apron and gold-framed glasses. "Aunt Debbie. Mom's sister. She makes a bundle for the Arts Council on this event. Dad claims she makes the most off him."

"Your dad does like his desserts."

"So do his sons, but the chocolate also makes terrific gifts for vendors and contractors. And Aunt Debbie knows it." He lifted a hand and waved at his aunt, grinning. "See how her eyes lit up? It's not because she adores her nephew. It's my wallet that makes her happy. That woman's a barracuda for the Arts Council."

Abby grinned and cocked her head. "I thought she was the guru."

"Guru, barracuda. I could think of other names, including chocolate queen. Wait until you taste her lava bites. Come on." He tugged her hand onto the wheelchair handle and put his on top. "Let's say hello and see if we can finagle a sample or two."

Abby fell in step beside her daughter, acutely aware of Brady's hand over hers. She couldn't help wondering if he was being Brady the nice guy, the giver who loved Christmas, or if his attention was really for her, Abby the woman, not Abby the project.

Did he have any idea what he was doing to her?

She was crazy in love with him, the man with a heart as big as his body. Crazy was probably the key word.

"Brady!" His aunt came around the counter to give him a hug. "Loved the TV interview. Brilliant on your part, I'd say. How's it working?"

"Great so far."

"Any takers on the reward?"

"No."

She patted his arm. "Don't give up. Someone knows something and the truth will eventually come out."

"I hope it happens before they destroy anything else."

"So do I, honey." Debbie stepped back as if assessing the woman with Brady. "You must be Abby."

"Oh, sorry," Brady said. "I thought the two of you had probably met."

"Not yet, but I'd say it's time."

"Oh, because of the home makeover," Abby said. Of course. That must be what Debbie meant. "Brady's been very kind to us."

"Kind." Debbie's eyes sparkled. "Yes, I imagine so, but from the looks of you two, I'd say kindness wasn't the only thing."

Abby's pulse stuttered. Really? Was she serious?

Floundering, Abby glanced at Brady and found his electric-blue eyes on her. A swarm of emotions buzzed inside her. Confusion. Longing. Hope. And most of all, an overpowering love.

Oh, but she hadn't meant to love him. Hadn't wanted to ever love anyone again. Love hurt too much.

Lila's voice broke the tension. "Are you the chocolate queen?"

Debbie laughed and adjusted her glasses. "I guess I am. Would you like a sample?"

"Yes, please!" Lila clapped her hands in delight and

the moment passed, though Abby couldn't get Debbie's remark out of her head.

Armed with a bakery box, they roamed the festival, sampling goodies. Jostling friends and neighbors, Brady shared warm greetings and banter with practically everyone. With him at her side, Abby felt a part of the town in a way she never had before. He was a magnet, not only because of his superior size but because of his friendliness.

Abby realized how seldom she'd done more than say hello to people she didn't know. At the diner, she knew the names and food choices of the regulars, but she never took the time to know them the way Brady did.

No wonder she was lonely.

"Give me two boxes of mixed truffles," Brady said to the man behind the table. To Abby, he said, "Want a few boxes for the other women at the diner? Jan, Charla, Fran?"

"Oh, I—" She frowned. She'd love to give something this lovely and extravagant to her friends, but the expense worried her. "Last year Lila and I baked cookies."

"Great idea, too, but you're pretty tied up at the house this year." He took one of the white-capped truffles and waved it under her nose. "Running tab, remember? Buy everything that appeals to you. The money goes to a good cause."

A good cause. Like her? "Well—"

Brady said to the clerk. "Four more boxes, please."

"Brady!"

He laughed. "Stop fussing. This is supposed to be fun."

Fun to him. Misery to her. She was a beggar.

But her coworkers would adore the truffles, and she and Lila *were* occupied this year with the house.

"Mommy," Lila said, tugging at her coat sleeve. "There's my teacher." Stretching up high to be noticed, she waved her little arm in excitement. "Miss Christina!"

Across the room, Christina somehow heard the small,

childish voice and turned, waving. When her gaze landed on Abby, she smiled, then turned back to the rows of chocolate.

"I love my teacher," Lila said.

The reminder cut Abby to the bone. How was she going to break the news to her child that she was no longer wanted at Christina's day care?

"Hey, why the long face? Did I do something wrong?" Brady dipped down to look in her eyes. "Are you mad about the truffles? You don't have to take them if you hate the idea."

She put a hand on his arm to stop the flow of worry. "The truffles are great. They'll love them."

"Then what happened? One minute you're laughing and the next you look as if your dog died."

"Nothing. Really." She pretended to study the array of cheesecakes. Her day-care issues were not his problem.

Brady put his fingertips against her back and leaned in. "You sure?"

She forced a smile. "Positive."

An older gentleman in an electric wheelchair pulled alongside and spoke to Lila. "Didn't I see this pretty little girl on television?"

Lila's face wreathed in pleasure. "My mommy, too. And Bwady. At our new house."

"How ya doin', J.D.?" Brady asked, offering a hand to shake. "Abby, you know J.D., don't you?"

"Hi, J.D. We've missed you at the diner lately." Southwestern omelet, Abby thought, with lots of *picante*. How pathetic that his order was the only thing she'd ever discussed with the man.

"Had a hospital stay, but I'm up and going again now." Thin as a rake with the bony arms and fingers to match, J.D. battled the aftereffects of a stroke.

"Glad to hear it," Brady said. "Anything you need?"

"Nah, nah, you've done enough for us." J.D. turned his focus to Abby and Lila. "You ladies are very fortunate to have Brady in your corner. He does wonders for this town."

"Now, J.D.," Brady started, shaking his head.

The old man waved a boney hand. "I keep my ear to the ground. I know what's going on."

Brady sidestepped the compliment, but Abby caught the drift.

Like many others past and present, she was his project. Once the house was finished, he'd move on to the next needy soul.

She had to be smart, to guard her heart—what was left of it. She was no longer a lonely teenager wishing for a Prince Charming. She was a grown woman with a child. And not a thing to offer anyone.

Oh, but the sneaky Christmas spirit made her dream of things she shouldn't.

Chapter Fourteen

Santa Claus didn't have anything on him.

Brady loaded a wrapped box containing the kitchen play set into the back of his truck along with a half-dozen other gifts. Dawg looked at him through the back glass as if he knew who the toys were for.

"A kid needs Christmas presents," Brady said to the affable canine face.

"You're talking to your dog in the middle of town. You've got to get more friends."

Brady spotted his sister on the sidewalk outside Bland's Department Store, a shopping bag over one arm, the sun shining on her flippy dark hair and a grin on her petite face.

"Allison, hi. What's up?"

"I could ask you the same. Last year you bribed me and Jaylee into doing all the shopping for your home-makeover recipients."

"Yeah, well, I had a little time."

She scoffed. "Since when? Mom says you haven't slept eight hours in so long, she's worried about your driving."

"I'm catching up." He motioned toward the gifts. "Want to help me with the rest?"

Her eyes widened. "There are more?"

Brady frowned. He'd already purchased the art set and now a few extras today. Had he gone overboard?

Nah, no such thing at Christmas.

"Not many. A few." He opened the truck door. "Coming?"

Allison hopped in the cab, chattering about everything under the sun, but especially her fiancé and the wedding they'd put off until spring. When they stopped in front of the Texas Rose Boutique, she fell silent.

"What are you buying in here?"

"Already bought. Angela's wrapping them."

"You didn't answer my question. This is a women's store, not a toy store."

"Well, my mom and sisters and Abby need presents under the tree, too."

"Abby?" His sister's dark eyes studied him for several long seconds. "What's going on, Brady?"

"What do you mean, what's going on? Come on, sis. Give me a break. It's Christmas."

"Granted, you love Christmas, and you're a born rescuer especially this time of year."

"I am?"

Allison laughed. "We all see it, Brady, even if you don't. That's why Dad made you COO. When things go wrong, as they always do at some point on every job, Brady jumps in to fix the problem. Even Dawg is a rescue!"

"I never thought of myself like that." He'd figured dad put the managerial job on him so he could be at his throat all the time, not because he saw his strengths.

"The Christmas home makeover is your biggest rescue of the year. That's why you love it so much." Allison studied him and then shrugged. "But this year is different. *You're* different. More personal. Like Abby is more than the latest recipient of Operation Christmas Makeover. You aren't rescuing Abby anymore, you're caring for her."

"No—" He stopped, pondering. "Maybe."

His sister's eyes lit up. "I think you're falling in love with her."

"What? No." But even as he denied the truth, he thought his sister might be right. "She's…"

Allison's look seemed to know more than he did. "Special?"

"Well, yeah."

"We all think so, too, Brady. Even though she's quiet, she fits with us. We like her." Allison flashed her engagement diamond in the sunlight. "Falling in love is a good thing."

Brady blew out a breath. "It's only a couple of presents, Allison. Christmas gifts. Don't make a mountain out of it. I don't think I'm ready for…that."

Her dark eyebrows lifted. "Are you sure?"

Brady opened the door and stepped out into the cold sunlight, reeling with the thoughts and emotions shooting through his body.

Allison was right about one thing. Abby meant more to him than the average housing project. He felt good when he was with her. Energized. Happy.

Maybe he *was* falling in love.

And maybe that wasn't a bad thing.

Abby heard voices in the living room, one in particular, and the sound of Lila's giggle let her know Brady had come to visit his parents.

She refused to believe he'd come to see her, though the night of the parade had been wonderful. She'd had fun, laughed and shopped and grown a hot cocoa mustache to match her daughter's. When they'd arrived home, Brady had kissed her good-night with such sweetness she wanted to believe it meant something more than a casual date.

"You take things too seriously," she reminded herself.

Hadn't she always? Men kissed women for no reason other than they'd had a nice time and they wanted to. She'd kissed boys in high school and didn't even remember their names! "Don't read too much into a good-night kiss."

Or any of the other things he did that made her feel important. Brady made everyone feel important. It was the Buchanon way.

She twirled a length of silver ribbon around a box wrapped in blue paper, secured a label on which she'd written "from Abby and Lila," and added the gift to the small stack on the end of her bed.

Resisting a fluff in the mirror, she scooped up the gifts and headed into the living room.

Brady crouched in the entry between two large poinsettias, a red-and-green wreath on the door at his back, his arms loaded with bags and boxes, talking to her daughter. "And this one is for your mom, but it's a secret surprise." He lowered his voice. "Can you hide it under the tree so she won't know?"

"Yes," Lila whispered, clearly intrigued by the shiny red box.

So was Abby.

"Brady, you shouldn't have done that."

"Oops. Busted." He stretched to his height and said, "She's sneaky. I didn't hear her coming."

"Because you were too busy conspiring with my innocent daughter." She perched a hand on her hip, amused... and attracted. He looked so appealing, like a big Celtic Santa in jeans and brown leather jacket.

"It's nothing much," he said with a shrug. "I was feeling Santa-ish and couldn't stop myself."

"You never can."

Amusement crinkled the corners of his eyes. "Is that a bad thing?"

Only to my heart.

"You're spoiling my daughter." *And I can't give her all this stuff next year. She has to learn that money doesn't grow on trees. Not for a woman who works at the local diner.* He scared her, this man who couldn't seem to understand her fear of his generosity.

"Ah, come on, Ab. It's Christmas. Don't be Scrooge."

Karen came in from the patio carrying a potted plant, her usually coifed hair wind ruffled. "I thought I heard your voice. Staying for dinner?"

"Can't. I'm working on Abby's house tonight." He went to the merrily blinking tree and dumped the stack of gifts next to a mound of others.

The house telephone rang and Karen answered. "For you, Abby. Someone returning your call."

Tension leaped up into her shoulders. She had calls in to several individuals who provided child care in their homes. None was a school, but each came well recommended as someone who cared about children.

With Christmas break only days away, her time was running out.

"Thanks." She took the cordless and stepped around the counter into the kitchen for privacy. "Hello."

Please, Lord. Let this be the right place.

Brady stewed all the way to Abby's almost complete home. He'd overheard her phone conversation. She was searching for a new babysitter for Lila. Huckleberry Play School had kicked her out.

When she'd come back into the living room, expression hangdog, he'd gone to her. "Why didn't you tell me?"

"Tell you what?" she'd hedged. She'd actually hedged. With *him*!

"I overheard, Abby. Why didn't you say something?"

She'd crossed her arms and lowered her voice so Lila wouldn't hear. "Because…it's not your problem."

His temper had flared like an emergency torch on a dark night. He hadn't said another word, but he'd thought plenty, and a few minutes later, he'd left before his temper got the best of him.

Now, he tromped down on the gas pedal, his fingers gripping the steering wheel tight enough to hurt.

Not his problem? How could he be there for her if she shut him out? Lila was important. *She* was important. Why did she always have to carry the weight of the world by herself?

He had a half a thought to call Christina, but she'd likely tell him the matter was not his business. Just as Abby had done.

The truck's speedometer shot to sixty. He eased off the pedal and whispered a prayer to get his anger under control.

Maybe Lila and Abby *weren't* his business. Maybe he only imagined Abby had feelings for him beyond the building project. She was grateful, yes, but she'd never once made the overtures. All the effort had been on his part. He'd invited her to dinner at his house. He'd initiated the kisses, the date to the parade, the lunches at the diner. Even the Christmas gifts were purchased over her protests.

He thumped his forehead on the steering wheel. "Idiot. She's trying to get the message through your thick skull and you refused to see it."

Abby liked him. She appreciated his work on her home. But that was where the relationship ended. She didn't want him in her business. Or in her life, for that matter. People who cared about each other shared the ups as well as the downs. That's what family did.

Okay, so he wasn't family. He was only the home builder. End of story. He could deal with that, would have to deal with it, though the truth stung more than he'd have liked. He was a big boy. He could take rejection.

He pulled into the driveway of the new construction. His brothers were already there, bless them. Even Quinn's truck was parked outside, evidence that he'd been bitten by the Christmas spirit. Lila had gotten to the grouchy brother, too.

Lila. The little girl had touched the whole family with her valiant spirit and sunny disposition. They'd seen the rigorous exercise Abby put her through each day and the discomfort she endured without complaint. Even the one time she'd cried from the pain of a new exercise and Abby had cried with her, she'd said, "It's okay, Mommy."

Abby didn't know he'd overheard that conversation or that he'd wanted to cry with them. The little girl had been through too much.

An idea came to him and he thought, "Why not?"

No matter how Abby felt about him, she wanted the best for her daughter, and so did he.

He fished out his cell phone and tapped in his mother's number.

By the time Abby arrived, his temper had cooled, he had a plan in place and was stirring the pink paint for Lila's princess room.

Nail guns popped in adjoining rooms and Quinn one-armed a roller up and down the front bathroom wall. Abby had chosen colors as quiet as her nature. In this case, sea-foam green.

"This is beautiful, Brady." Abby stood inside the door to Lila's room, where Brady worked alone. The princess room was his project and his only. He wanted to do this for Lila.

Three walls remained covered in gray drywall primer, but the east wall shone with fresh princess pink.

"Should I grab a roller and help in here or move on to another room?"

Brady put aside the roller and said, "I want to talk to you about something first."

She perched her fists on the hips of her worn work jeans, expression cautious. "You sound serious. Is everything okay?"

"I hope so." Brady wiped excess paint from his hands and pulled a sheet of paper from the pocket of his coveralls. Abby moved to his side to look.

"Let me be clear." His voice sounded cranky even to him. "I don't want to be involved where I'm not wanted. If you think I'm butting into your business, I'll back off."

At his tone, she looked up, worried. "I'm not sure what you mean. Are you mad at me about something?"

"No."

"Yes, you are." Her eyes searched his. "What did I do?" She touched his sleeve. "Tell me."

"You said Lila's day care wasn't my problem."

"It isn't," she said quietly.

She was the most frustrating woman on the planet. "What if I want it to be? What if my family and I *want* to help? Come on, Abby, work with me here."

She pulled back, frowning. "Why would you?"

After all they'd done together in the past few months, she didn't trust him. "Why can't you accept help at face value? Because people care about you!" He was getting riled again. "Do you always have to question everyone's motives?"

"Yes!"

Her response stunned him. He quieted. "Why?"

But he knew the answer. Her life had been a journey of disappointments, letdowns and rejection.

She glanced toward the pink wall, mouth pinched tight. "People don't do something for nothing."

"Maybe that's your experience, but it's not true. Not always. Stop expecting the worst out of everyone. Out of me. I'm not going to hurt you, Abby."

Brady saw her hesitation and watched her struggle with

some inner fear. He waited her out, letting her battle it through. She gnawed her bottom lip, looked at her feet and then at him.

Finally, her shoulders relaxed. "You've been more than good to us, Brady. I'm sorry if I hurt your feelings. I didn't want to burden you with anything else."

"You're not a burden. You're—" He caught himself, breathed in the scent of paint and drywall mud, and tried again. He was crazy about her. Didn't she understand? "I thought we were more than builder and client."

Okay, he was putting his heart out there for her to drill with a nail gun.

She stilled.

"Are we?" The words were soft and incredulous.

His voice tendered. "I don't go around kissing clients."

A subtle shift occurred, a chink in her high wall of distrust and pride. Her mouth tilted the slightest bit. "I'm glad to hear that."

He decided to throw caution to the wind.

"I spend extra time with you because I want to be in your company. What I do on my personal time has nothing to do with this building. It's you." Couldn't she see that she meant more to him than a few boards and a coat of paint? "If I'm way out of line here and you're not interested, now might be a good time to tell me."

Eyes deer-in-the-headlights wide, as if the admission scared her to death, she whispered, "I'm interested."

A smile bloomed in Brady's chest. Now they were getting somewhere.

"Good answer. Come here." He opened his arms and she walked into him. Cradling her gently, he asked, "Will you stop second-guessing everything I do for you?"

She tilted her face up. "I'll try."

All right. A step in the right direction.

"Then look at this schedule the family and I put together and be happy. Don't argue. Be happy."

She tipped back, dubious. "A schedule for what?"

"Lila. The family volunteered to look after her when you're at work."

"Are you serious?"

He flexed his arm in a quick squeeze and loosened his hold to show her the schedule.

"There you go again. Yes, I'm serious. Until you can find the perfect place for day care, the Buchanons will take charge of the princess. Easy peasy." He tapped the paper. "Everyone who could took a spot for the next month. After that, we'll start again."

"I can't believe this. She loves your family and feels secure with them. They understand her needs. This is… perfect, but you don't have time for—"

He put a hand over her mouth. "We'll make time. We love her, too, Ab. She's fun."

"She's also a lot of work."

"Aren't we all?"

At that, she smiled her wide, full-mouthed smile that turned his world brighter. "I can't believe you people are real. Sometimes, I think this is a dream. I don't know how to thank you or what to do to repay you. You're just so—so—"

Brady didn't know who moved first, but Abby had her hands on his face and was kissing him. *She* kissed *him.*

The popping nail guns faded away and he didn't notice or care that his hair was flecked with pink paint or that his brothers were mere steps away in the next rooms. For the moment, Abby was his world.

Chapter Fifteen

The days leading up to Christmas were the happiest Abby could ever remember. Embraced by the Buchanon family and courted by Brady, she lived in a dream world. Sometimes late at night, she'd awaken, heart pounding in panic that the dream would end and she'd come crashing to the ground, brokenhearted and alone again.

More than anything, she feared for Lila, who sparkled in the Buchanons' loving attention. If the romance ended, her little girl would face the kind of disappointment Abby never wanted her to feel. Rejection. The belief that she wasn't quite good enough.

But in the light of day as her beautiful home neared completion, and she and Brady spent hours together, Abby put aside her fears, determined to bask in every beautiful moment.

Overwhelmed with gratitude, she rose early to clean the Buchanons' house and do as much extra for them as she could squeeze in to her crowded day. Though Karen insisted it wasn't necessary, she wanted to. She needed to. She didn't have money for big gifts, but she knew how to work. When she'd tried to pay them for looking after Lila, they'd refused.

"Spend your money on things for the new house," Karen had said.

She'd never met anyone like them in her life. But the savings gave her money to buy Christmas gifts, and she enjoyed a marvelous day off shopping with Charla.

On Christmas Eve, she and Brady attended a peaceful, uplifting candlelight service, and then shared a late supper of finger foods and chicken gumbo at the Buchanons' afterward.

Understandably overexcited, Lila had trouble settling down for the night. Finally Abby said, "Time for bed, baby. Santa Claus won't come while you're awake."

"Will you wead me a story?" Lila's droopy eyes kept returning to the pile of gifts under the tree. Abby had let her open one, a pair of fleece candy-cane pajamas that she now wore.

"Sure." She lifted her bath-scented daughter into her arms.

Karen offered a book. "I used to read this to my kids every Christmas Eve."

"My favorite," Brady said. *The Night before Christmas.*

"Mine, too." Something else they had in common. "I've read it to Lila every Christmas, but I think this is the first year she'll remember."

"You come, too, Bwady," Lila said. "Wead with me. Mommy's a good weader."

Smiling, Brady looked to Abby for confirmation, and with her heart skipping too many beats, she said, "Come on."

Once Lila was tucked into bed, Abby sat on the edge next to her. Brady, his powerful body dwarfing the space, knelt at the headboard close to Lila.

As they took turns reading, Abby listened to his manly voice, realizing this was the first time in Lila's life a man had read her to sleep. For a few sweet seconds, while Lila's coffee-dark eyes adored Brady, Abby let the thoughts flow, pretending this was her family and Brady was Lila's father.

The vision in her head was so strong and poignant, it pierced her. Being with the Buchanons had shown her the things she'd missed and the things in life that really mattered. God. Family. Love. She wanted all of them...with Brady. Was she foolish to believe something so grand could happen? After this time with him, after hope and love and joy had buoyed up inside her, if Brady walked away, she didn't how she'd ever recover.

"'Happy Christmas to all, and to all a good night,'" Brady declared, and clapped the book shut. "Ready to say your prayers?"

Abby's heart clutched when Lila folded her tiny hands over her red-and-white pj's while Brady led her in a simple, heartfelt prayer. At the *amen* he leaned in and kissed her baby's forehead. "Sleep tight, princess."

"'Night, Bwady." Lila heaved a deep, sleepy breath. "Bwady?"

He exchanged an indulgent look with Abby, probably suspecting as she did that Lila was procrastinating going to sleep on this exciting night.

"What?"

"I wuv you."

Brady brushed Lila's dark hair back from her face, his hand dwarfing the tiny head, his too-handsome face serious. "I love you, too, princess."

Touched and troubled that her baby was getting in over her head exactly like her mama, Abby glanced away from the endearing sight. She kissed Lila good-night, and the adults left the room together, snapping off the light at the door.

In the dim, shadowy hall with Brady's arm brushing hers, she said, "I think I'll call it a night, too." She tiptoed up, hands on his broad, capable shoulders and kissed him lightly. "Good night, Brady."

His smile tilted the edges of his mouth. "Good night."

He didn't move, though. He remained in the wide hallway, close enough for his warm apple-cider scent to fill her senses.

He looked as if he wanted to say more but after three heartbeats, he turned and started down the hall. The need to be as brave and bold as her daughter throbbed in Abby's throat. She wanted to call out to him, call him back. Three words she longed to say, but fear and uncertainty held them captive.

When he disappeared around the corner, Abby whispered to the emptiness, "I love you, Brady."

Christmas morning was a madhouse.

Warm, cozy and crowded, the Buchanon home was redolent of tempting smells—cinnamon, turkey and apple spice with a side note of peppermint. And noise. Lots of happy noise.

Dawson, in his gentle baritone, read the Christmas story from the Bible while the gathered family drank eggnog, cocoa or coffee and rubbed the sleep from their eyes. The three children, still in pajamas, loitered beneath the tree and anxiously awaited the big moment when they could dive into the mound of gifts.

"Santa came, Mama. He came!" Lila's eyes were as wide as saucers.

He had, indeed. Abby knew the Buchanons were a little Christmas crazy but she hadn't imagined anything this extravagant. Saying "you shouldn't have" was about as useful as telling Brady to grow shorter.

Abby perched on the edge of the couch. Brady handed her a cup of eggnog. "Thanks, I love this stuff even if it's überfattening."

"You have nothing to worry about. Scoot." He crowded out his sister to sit beside Abby. Allison winked at him and snuggled her cowboy on the other side. Abby didn't mind a bit that they were jammed together like sardines.

When the moment finally arrived, Dan took his place beneath the tree to hand out gifts.

"Need a little help this year, Brady. The family keeps growing."

"Like the business," Dawson said.

"And we're thankful for both." Karen raised a mug as if in toast.

Brady set aside his half-finished eggnog and unwound himself from the couch to join his father.

"My right-hand man," Dan said, and they hugged in that smiling, back-patting way of men. "Couldn't get along without you, son."

"Merry Christmas, Dad."

Throughout the gift exchange, the two men laughed and teased in the affectionate Buchanon way. Their relationship bewildered Abby, but on this day the father and son were at peace. For Brady's sake, she prayed the truce continued.

While Bing Crosby dreamed of a white Christmas from SiriusXM, paper and ribbons flew, and the recipients, especially the overexcited children, squealed in delight. Abby vacillated between pleasure at her daughter's joy and the painful awareness that Lila had never before had more than three small gifts under the tree. Her best, it seemed, had been inadequate, because today there were so many she couldn't keep count. She was more thankful than ever that she'd been able to buy each of the Buchanons a little something.

Her favorite part of the morning was watching the interactions between the family members. The love that flowed in the room was almost palpable. Even Brady and Dan seemed to truly care about each other, and the usually solemn Quinn teased his sisters and snitched tempting morsels from the kitchen.

This was the kind of family she'd once thought only existed on television or in books. Families that stuck together and helped each other, that loved and laughed even when they disagreed. They were big and loud and wonderful and she loved them. She deeply desired this kind of life for her daughter and, yes, for herself, too.

Heart full and amazed, Abby sat on the floor beside the fireplace, surrounded by mounds of colorful paper and gifts. Brady's Dawg curled against the hearth, asleep in all the commotion.

"You gonna open those presents or keep them till next year?" Brady knelt next to her, leaving his dad to hand out the stockings.

"I'm watching Lila. This is the first year she's really understood what was going on."

Enamored with the play kitchens from Brady, Lila and Amber had already started a game of "house" with the tea sets from Allison and the dolls from Karen and Dan. Giggling and jabbering, Lila scooted her walker with ease from stove to stove and balanced her belly against the crossbar to "cook."

"Incredible kid." Brady watched Lila with a soft smile. "Amazing the way she adapts. Look at her."

Pride and love filled Abby's chest. "She finds a way, but really, Brady, you shouldn't have bought so much—"

He placed two fingers over her lips. "Don't say it. Anything goes on Christmas. Including your gifts. Open something before we think you don't like them."

"Oh." She hadn't thought of that. She simply hadn't wanted to look like a greedy, needy pig. "You haven't opened yours, either."

"Let's do it!" He ripped into his with the same abandon as the children. From her, he opened a bottle of men's Eternity.

"How did you know this is my favorite?" He unscrewed the lid and sniffed.

"I like the way it smells on you."

"Yeah?" He seemed pleased by that. He slapped a little on his face and leaned close. "What do you think?"

What did she think? She thought he was gorgeous and wonderful, cologne or not.

She sniffed his cheek with melodramatic exaggeration. "I think I have great taste in cologne."

"Wait till you open yours. You'll laugh."

Abby took her time, treasured every ribbon, which she set aside in an empty box, admired the pretty paper and then delighted in each gift inside. A scarf, a wallet, a CD, things for her new house, a sweater, and from Brady, a perfume set she'd fallen in love with on one of their window-shopping adventures. She had spritzed her wrist and neck, and the rest of the evening he'd told her how good she smelled.

She didn't laugh that they'd given each other cologne. It made her feel closer to him.

Abby closed her eyes and held the bottle to her nose. "I love this. Thank you."

"Put some on." His quiet rumble was temptingly close.

She did. The light floral-and-sandalwood fragrance filled the air and her senses.

Lila looked up from her play. "Mommy smells yummy, right, Bwady?"

"Yes, she does." When Abby only smiled in return, he said, "I suspect your Christmas is usually quieter. Feeling overwhelmed yet?"

"A little, but in a good way. Thank you for the gift. For… all of this." How did she express the depth and breadth of her emotions to a man who'd always had this kind of Christmas?

"What do you say we take a run over to your house?"

"Now?"

"I want to show you something." He stood and pulled her up by both hands. "Lila's having a blast with Amber, and dinner isn't until two."

"But I'm helping your mom with the meal."

"Mom," he called to where his mother leaned on the bar talking to Charity. They were waiting for a Skype call from Charity's husband, a career military pilot. "Can you spare Abby for a few minutes?"

"Of course."

"We won't be gone long," Abby said, feeling a little guilty about running out on the work, though they'd done most of the dinner preparations last night.

"Take your time. It's Christmas."

"Okay, then, if you're sure. Let me get my coat." She whirled her new scarf around her neck and kissed her daughter goodbye. Entranced by toys, candy and a play-mate, Lila hardly noticed Abby was leaving.

When they arrived at the house, now almost complete and looking new and inviting beneath the cold, clear Christmas sky, Brady handed her a small gold-wrapped box. Inside was a key ring bearing her name and a set of keys.

"Is this—?" She glanced toward the red entry door.

"It is." He withdrew a packet of papers from inside his jacket and handed them to her. "Merry Christmas, Abby." Grinning, he spread his arms dramatically. "Welcome to your new home. The outside still needs a few finishing touches, but the inside is ready to go."

"But how is that possible? Two days ago—"

"A few guys and gals did a little overtime." He lifted a

shoulder as if what they'd done was no big deal. "Maybe a lot of overtime."

"They worked on Christmas Eve? For me?"

"They wanted you to take possession today, a Christmas present from me and the crew."

"I don't know what to say." Her hand trembled as she put the key in the lock and opened the door. She'd been inside dozens of times but today was different. Today the home was hers.

They stepped into the smell of new wood, fresh paint and lemon cleaner.

All evidence of construction that had been here as recently as two days ago had disappeared. The paint cans, two-by-sixes and drop cloths were gone. Electrical outlets were covered, knobs were in place on the cabinets and doors, and every room had been immaculately cleaned, windows polished to a shine and wood trim rubbed with oil. Even a few pieces of furniture now graced the rooms.

"Oh, Brady," she breathed, gazing around her home. Her beautiful, beautiful home. Tears of joy prickled the backs of her eyelids. "Unbelievable."

Abby slid her palms along the cold granite countertops, turned the nickel faucets on and off, peeked in the stainless-steel refrigerator.

"Empty," Brady said, and they both laughed for no reason except pleasure.

They roamed the living room, tested the thermostat and gazed out the sparkling-clean dining room windows toward a backyard bare of plants except for two leafless red maples that had survived the bulldozer. In spring, grass would grow again. She could plant flowers. Karen had already offered starts from her gorgeous backyard.

This was perfect.

Inside Lila's room, Abby spun in a circle, heart spilling over, beside herself with happiness. To accommodate Lila's walker, the room was intentionally sleek and streamlined, but on the wall above a pink-and-white canopied bed, some artistic hand had painted a crown and the words, *Princess Lila*. Gauzy curtains draped the windows, which were framed in castle-turret wallpaper. It was the kind of room every little girl dreamed of.

"This is… I don't even have words. She will be so happy."

Brady's eyes sparkled. "What about her mom?"

"I love it. You know I do."

"Good. Good." He moved to the window and pushed aside a pink curtain.

Abby ran her fingers lightly over the girly white bedside table, admiring the pink lamp. "I thought you'd want a reporter present when you turned over the keys. For publicity."

"She'll wait until the remaining furniture is in and the exterior is complete." He looked at her over one very broad shoulder. "I wanted today to be the two of us. No audience. No TV. No other family. And definitely not client and builder. Just Brady and Abby. You and me. Alone."

Abby's breath caught at the hushed tone in his voice.

He turned to face her, placing his hands on the windowsill behind him. For a sweet, aching moment their gazes locked until Abby looked down at the pink crystals dangling from the lamp. She was as wishful as a fairy tale.

Brady stirred, and she felt him move toward her, the giant of a man who moved with athletic grace. Abby's pulse thrummed with wild hope and terrible fear. Not of Brady but of her own needy heart and past mistakes.

He took hold of her shoulders with gentle hands and stood as quiet as a stone until she looked up and babbled, "You've worked so hard and done so much, I—"

He cut her off with a shake of his head, saying, "I'd do it all over again in a heartbeat. You're a special woman, Abby Webster."

Her mouth curved. "You're a special man. Just look at this fabulous place. No one else could have done what you did. No one would have wanted to."

"This isn't about the house. Or me. I'm talking about you, the woman who works too hard and champions her special child, who bought gifts for my family when I know you need the money." When she started to deny the truth, he put a finger over her lips and stopped her. "I know about the hours you and Lila volunteer on the hospital children's wing—I was there, remember? And about the time a mother and her five kids stayed with you to escape an abusive relationship."

"Where did you learn about that?"

"This is Gabriel's Crossing. People talk. But that's beside the point."

"What is the point?"

He cupped her cheek, smile tender. "The point is, I love you."

The admission was both beautiful and scary. She nodded, the words she wanted to say thick in her throat.

A battle raged inside Abby's chest as she fought against past experiences. Warren had said he loved her, too. But when times turned hard, so did his heart. Exactly like the other people in her past. Love was conditional.

Intellectually, Abby knew Warren and Brady were as different as fire and water, but the vulnerable part of her was afraid. The scared child who'd been shuffled from foster home to foster home, the awkward misfit who was prey to cruel gibes in school and the jilted pregnant fiancée still lived and ached inside the independent woman. She wanted Brady with all her heart but the coward inside held back.

Yet, Brady had put no conditions on this house or her. He'd given her a place to live with his family, a babysitting service and the best Christmas ever. Was that love?

No, that couldn't be right. He'd given home makeovers to other people, as well. Love had to be…more.

"Hey," Brady said softly. "Are you going to leave me hanging?"

She shook her head, throat dry as chalk. "Of course not. I—"

"Don't say it if you don't mean it."

Head down, she moistened dry lips and murmured, "I do."

He tipped her chin up, blue, blue eyes questioning.

She nodded. "Yes."

The brilliance of his smile was worth everything. He hugged her to him, his heart pounding and pounding in her ear. Her own heart pounded, too.

Even in the midst of joy, an earthquake shook her insides and the voice in her head shouted a warning. Love was temporary. Love exacted a painful price.

She pushed the voice down, down, down and clasped tightly to the hope that this time love meant forever.

Chapter Sixteen

The week following Christmas Abby began moving her stored belongings into the new home a little at a time. After business hours, Brady and his brothers did the heavy lifting, and if she and Brady spent too much time grinning at each other instead of working, she couldn't help it. She loved him desperately.

By New Year's Eve, the bulk of the donated furniture had arrived. Abby had spent most of her day off arranging and rearranging for the sheer thrill of it.

"You and Lila could sleep here tonight if you wanted," Brady said as he plunked a cardboard box on the countertop.

She shook her head. "I want to start the year off in my new home. Tomorrow, New Year's Day, Lila and I will bring over our things from your parents' house and settle in. It's...symbolic. A new year, a new start, a new house."

"Can't argue with sentiment." He dragged open the box flaps and lifted out a plate. "Where do these go?"

"Dishwasher. They've been in storage long enough to get dirty."

"A guy would wipe them on his jeans and stick them in the cabinet."

She laughed. "You would not."

"Probably not. Mom would hurt me."

"So would I." Plates clinked as they unboxed the dishes. The set was small and inexpensive, but she liked the clean white design.

As they loaded the dishwasher together, he said, "We still on for tonight?"

"Absolutely. Can't wait." She inspected a teacup for chips. "I usually spend New Year's Eve at home with Lila. We watch a movie, eat some popcorn and she falls asleep long, long before the ball drops. Mostly, I do, too."

He laughed. "I've done that a few times myself. But not tonight. I want to take my lady on the town."

His lady. Brady's easy acceptance of their new relationship made her feel vulnerable. How long would one of the town's most eligible bachelors be interested in ordinary Abby from the diner? Would she still be his lady this time next year? Or even next week after she and Lila were moved in and no longer a Christmas project?

Abby fought off the negative thoughts. Since Christmas Day they'd driven her crazy. Twice, she'd had a nightmare. She'd been in a crowd of smiling, talking, happy people but none of them could see her. She'd been invisible. She'd seen Brady standing tall above the crowd. Happy and relieved, she waved and called out. His eyes met hers, but when she ran to embrace him, he'd turned away and left her alone, invisible again.

The Old Red Barn was a popular restaurant and events venue that specialized in music, steaks and New Year's Eve.

"Ever attended one of their New Year's Eve parties?" Brady asked as he held her elbow and guided her from the quickly filling gravel parking lot through the darkness to the brightly lit building.

"No."

"Me, either."

"Really?" She'd imagined him as a man who always had a date and never missed a party.

"I've been here for dinner but not on New Year's Eve. The steaks are great. Shrimp's good. Lobster rocks the world."

"I've never had lobster," she admitted.

"Want to try it?"

Abby grimaced. "It looks creepy."

He laughed. "Looks are deceiving. Except for yours. You look gorgeous tonight."

Abby had pressed the one dress she saved for special occasions, mostly funerals and weddings, a simple black sheath with a blue cardigan and black heels. The temperature hovered around freezing and a stiff north wind blew in another arctic front, but there was no way she'd wear the puffy red jacket on a New Year's Eve date no matter how cold she got. She refused to shiver.

"You look nice, too." *Really nice.* In a suit and tie, her Celtic warrior was a dream.

Inside the restaurant, quiet music played and candlelight lit the room in a golden, shadowy glow. The atmosphere felt romantic and elegant, though all that would change when the live band kicked off at nine and the party really began.

Brady gave his name to the hostess, who responded with a very warm smile and led them to a cozy table. With a flirtatious tilt of her head, the hostess glanced at Brady from beneath her eyelashes. "Is this suitable, Mr. Buchanon?"

"Great."

Abby tried not to be jealous. Brady was with her, but obviously other women, including the young hostess, noticed his good looks and Buchanon clout.

After she was seated, Abby said, "I feel a little guilty eating anywhere except the Buttered Biscuit."

"It's not open."

"Good point. Jan and Dave are off on their cruise."

"See? Even they're eating somewhere else. So, what sounds good? You going for that lobster?"

She'd make a fool of herself trying to eat something served in a shell. She looked over the menu. "Maybe the grilled salmon with lemon-infused quinoa. That sounds pretty fancy for a woman who serves burgers and meat loaf."

"I'm not a fancy kind of guy. I'm going for the herb-crusted beef tenderloin and garlic mashed."

"Sounds fancy to me."

"Steak and potatoes. Can't get more basic than that."

The waitress reappeared with their drinks and took their orders.

"I thought we might see some of your family here tonight."

"Still could. Nightlife in Gabriel's Crossing is limited, even on New Year's Eve."

"Allison said she and Jake were going to a friend's party. A Mexican fiesta, I think."

"And Mom and Dad were having some business friends over. The twins had dates but I didn't ask where they were going, and Jaylee had plans with friends. A concert, I think, down in Paris."

"It was nice of Charity to invite Lila to spend the night."

"She was staying home with the kids anyway and thought having Lila over would be fun for Amber. I heard rumors about popcorn, movies and a bubble-blowing contest."

Lila would love every minute of the sleepover even if she'd be cranky as a bear tomorrow from staying up too late.

"That accounts for everyone except Quinn," Abby said. "I hope he isn't alone."

Brady frowned. "He probably is. He didn't used to be a

loner but after the shooting, he withdrew from everything. When he finished college he took a job with a big firm in Dallas and moved away from all of us. Infuriated Dad."

"I'm sure."

"Yeah. By the time he moved home again, we thought he'd put the accident behind him."

"But he hasn't?"

"If anything he's gotten worse. He bought an old hunting cabin down on the river, and he'd rather be there than anywhere."

"Does he have a girlfriend?"

"Quinn? No. He'd scare a nice girl away."

"Was he always so reclusive and…?"

"Negative?" He smoothed the napkin onto his lap. "I forget you weren't around then. No, he wasn't. He was Mr. Big Man on Campus, the favorite son with the golden arm who was going to be a huge star in the NFL. He had an agent, a contract offer, the works. Everyone loved Quinn and he loved them, too." He fiddled with his fork. "All that changed with the accident."

"But he and Jake seem cordial when the family gets together."

"They are. The brothers had it in for Jake for a lot of years, but Allison loved him and we finally realized that forgiveness is better for everyone."

"Quinn forgave Jake for permanently damaging his arm?"

"He says he has. Sometimes I wonder if Quinn blames himself now that he doesn't have Jake to blame anymore."

"You worry about him."

"He's my brother. I love him. And, yeah, something is wrong, so I worry."

To hear a man talk so freely about love for his family touched her. "And you want to fix it."

He huffed softly. "You sound like Allison. She says I want to rescue everyone."

Did that include her?

The soft murmur of voices and gentle laughter filtered across the restaurant as waitstaff moved in quiet efficiency. The smell of steak and fresh, hot bread made Abby's mouth water while somewhere in the distance outside the restaurant a siren wailed.

The canned music kicked into Harry Connick Jr. crooning "Stardust."

"Are we still in Texas?" Brady joked.

"I think it's romantic."

He pumped his eyebrows. "Then I hope they play old Harry all night."

"I doubt that's going to happen since Boogie Salad takes the stage at nine."

Brady's eyes danced. "Crazy name for a band, but Boogie Salad is pretty good."

"You've heard them before?"

"YouTube. Checked them out before I made the reservation. They're a party band. Fun and energetic. They play a little bit of everything. Whatever the crowd wants."

Harry's smooth voice eased into "The Way You Look Tonight."

"Oh," Abby said, and sighed. "This is beautiful. His voice melts around the words."

"Melts? Should I be jealous?"

"No more than me."

"What does that mean?"

Abby blushed, the heat rushing up the back of her neck like warm water. "The hostess and the waitress were both flirting."

"Were they?"

She made a scoffing noise. "You know they were."

"You're the only one I'm interested in, Abby." His expression turned serious as he laced his fingers with hers atop the table. "I've never seen your hair down before."

"No?" Her hand went to the long waves that fell around her shoulders.

"It's beautiful." Above the flicker of a single candle, his blue eyes glowed with a soft, tender emotion, an emotion she felt, too. "Don't laugh, but I've had this crazy itch to take down your ponytail for a long time."

She didn't laugh. She couldn't. Her throat was too full. At the thought of Brady's wide fingers in her hair, a tingle raced over her skin. Tonight she felt like Cinderella at the ball, madly in love with her Prince Charming.

Please don't let the clock strike midnight.

"Abby," he started, lifting one of her fingers and then another. He sounded so serious.

"Yes?" Her pulse stuttered against her collarbone.

His cell phone interrupted. He leaned back in his chair and groaned. "This better not be work. Excuse me."

Abby sat back, too, sipped at her water and listened while Brady spoke into the receiver. He frowned. "What?"

When his eyes flicked to hers, she knew something was wrong.

Very slowly, she set her glass on the table. Condensation dampened her hands. She wiped the moisture on her napkin, aware that she was suddenly afraid and didn't know why.

Brady ended the call and stood with an abruptness that alarmed her.

"Brady?" She rose, too, fumbling for her handbag at her feet.

"We have to go." His face was set in harsh lines that no amount of candlelight could soften.

Fear prickled the hair on her arms. "What's wrong?"

He took her elbow.

"Brady, tell me. Is it Lila?" A mother's fear stole her

breath. She froze, refusing to move until he told her. "Is she all right?"

"Yes. Lila's fine."

Relief made her knees shake. Brady propelled her toward the door. "It's your house."

Something in his voice was terrible. He tossed money at the hostess and opened the exit door. A blast of frigid wind nearly knocked them down.

Alarm sounded in Abby's head. "My house?"

"It's on fire."

Sirens ripped the night in high-pitched cries of alarm as Brady raced from one side of town to the other. Abby hovered against the passenger door, her face stark in the dashboard lights, her posture rigid, arms crossed.

Brady could relate. A tight knot had his empty belly in a stranglehold.

"It'll be okay."

Abby turned her head. She no more believed the words than he did.

He bit down on his jaw. He'd make it be okay.

Abby gasped and leaned forward, palms braced on the dashboard. "Brady. Look. Oh, no."

He saw. Flames as high as the moon turned the night into day and obliterated the stars. And he and Abby weren't even in the neighborhood yet.

His belly sank lower, sick. Nauseated. *God, how could this happen?* To her, of all people.

He turned on First Street and accelerated hard down the empty pavement. In seconds, the truck bumped over the railroad tracks and into Abby's neighborhood.

The smell of smoke seeped into the cab. Abby made a small noise of distress and Brady wanted badly to be holding her instead of driving. She looked so alone huddled against the window.

He screeched to a halt a half a block away, Cedar Corner blocked by the fire engine, a rescue truck, police and a handful of gawkers.

They got out and ran toward the house, but Brady didn't have to be up close and personal to know they were too late.

The north wind whipped the flames into an inferno. Sparks shot hundreds of feet into the air, and the awful sound of hungry fire crackled and chewed through wood. The porch awning shuddered and a firefighter shouted.

Bunker-geared figures pulled back, massive hoses aimed toward the flames but impotent in the wind.

"What happened, Jason?" Brady said to the fire chief, the first uniformed person he encountered.

"Don't know yet and won't know much until the fire settles down. This one of yours?"

"I built it. It's Abby's new house."

The chief, face flickering gray and red in the flames, looked at Abby. "You're Brady's Christmas makeover?"

She nodded numbly, arms crossed tight and lips trembling.

Brady looped an arm around her. She was like a statue, stiff and unyielding, but he held fast. She wasn't a makeover.

"I'm sorry, ma'am. By the time my men arrived, the roof was involved and the garage was gone."

Brady heard what the chief wasn't saying. If the roof was gone, the rest of the house didn't have much chance.

"Let me know what you discover on the cause."

"Will do." The man spoke into his radio and moved away.

Abby's body quivered in the cold and from shock, too, he imagined. "It's too cold out here and neither of us is dressed for this kind of weather. You don't even have a coat. Come on."

"They can't save my house, can they?"

"No."

Her stiff resolve crumbled then. She turned to him, shattered, shaking, and the tears flowed down her smoke-smudged cheeks. "Oh, Brady. All your hard work for nothing."

She walked into his chest and held him as if he had the most to lose. As if he was the one who mattered.

"I'm so sorry, sweetheart. So sorry." He crushed her to him and gave comfort where he could. He smoothed her long, beautiful hair, the hair he'd wanted to touch for so long. But not like this. Never like this.

Her body quaked and he knew she was crying silent, brokenhearted sobs. Secret sobs she kept to herself. They sliced him to the core.

The news media arrived to film the destruction and interview the fire chief. Brady was grateful that they hadn't come to him. Abby didn't need a camera in her face.

Car doors slammed, and flames crackled and popped. The fire engine's pump hummed, loud enough to drown out speech. The front of the house gave way; fire ate into the wood until walls collapsed in a gust.

Heat mixed with frigid wind reached them in swirls. Brady unbuttoned his suit jacket and guided Abby's arms inside, against his body. "We should go."

She shook her head. "I can't. I can't."

Everything she owned except for the few items at his parents' home was inside the burning house, and he couldn't go in and get them for her.

They stood in the heat and cold, light and dark, huddled together watching the flames devour her dreams. One by one, except for Charity who'd blessedly remained at home with the children, his family arrived and stood silently with them as Abby's dream home burned to rubble.

Chapter Seventeen

New Year's Day didn't begin the way Brady had intended. Running on fumes, his eyes as red as embers and the smell of smoke still in his lungs, he staggered into his mother's kitchen at eleven.

"Did you sleep at all?" She slid a cup of coffee onto the bar.

"A few hours." He'd gone home, gone to bed, but sleep had been elusive. "Every time I closed my eyes, I saw Abby's house burning." And her face. He'd seen her devastated expression over and over. Even now, it tormented him.

"I don't think Abby slept much, either."

"How could this happen, Mom?" He stared morosely into the steaming coffee. "We've never had a fire. What could have gone wrong?"

His father entered the kitchen, his Buchanon Built cap and jacket a sign he'd been out and about. He reached for a coffee cup. "I'll tell you how it happened."

At his crisp tone, Brady swiveled on the bar chair. "Did you hear something?"

"The fire marshal arrives later, but Jason thinks the fire started in the garage near the hot-water tank."

"The tank? It was working fine when I checked it."

"*Near* the tank, Brady. Pay attention." Dan's tone hardened. "Someone messed up."

Brady was already shaking his head. "I don't think so, Dad. I was the last person in that house yesterday afternoon. And even before I let Abby start moving her things in, I had personally checked everything from plumbing to electrical plugs."

"You personally checked? Did you? Are you positive? Or were you more focused on Abby than on your job?"

Brady stiffened, temper crawling up the back of his neck. "What are you implying?"

"I don't imply. You know me better than that." Dan poked a finger in his direction. "Your negligence caused the fire."

"Dan!" Karen came around the end of the bar to face her husband. "You don't know that."

"Fires don't just happen, Karen. Someone causes them, especially in new construction. Someone didn't do his job correctly. A loose wire in an outlet. Lacquer thinner or paint rags left behind. An overloaded plug. Fire is preventable. This was Brady's project. His responsibility."

"That doesn't mean he was negligent."

"No?" Dan slammed his hand down on the bar. "It does to me."

Anger warred with the overwhelming sense that his father was right. Abby's house was his from ground up. He'd been in on every single element of the construction. If something had gone wrong, the fault was his. He *had* stored lacquer thinner cans in the garage. Even if he had an excuse, he knew better. Spontaneous combustion from rags or cans was real and a hot water tank, even across the room, could possibly spark and ignite the fumes.

"I'll make it right, Dad."

"I hope you had sense enough to have the house well insured."

Anger boiled up higher. He pushed it down. This was his fault, not his dad's. "I'll talk to the insurance adjuster today and start plans for the rebuild right away."

"Rebuild? We don't have time for a rebuild now."

He jolted, stunned. "We have to. Abby—"

Dan's voice rose. "You don't *have* to do anything on this house. It's a freebie, remember? No one is paying us a dime to rebuild."

Brady pushed his cold coffee aside. "Don't go there, Dad."

"You've strained us to the limit on this project already. The rebuild will have to wait."

Abby cried all the way to work. Exhausted, heartsick and guilt ridden, she didn't know what to do.

She'd heard the battle between father and son. The yelling.

The word *freebie* rolled over and over in her mind. Charity case. Freebie. They were the same thing. Both made her feel less than human. A weight, a nuisance, in the way.

After a full week of peace between Brady and his dad, they were at each other's throats again. Because of the house. Because of her.

She parked the car in back of the diner and patted makeup under her eyes before going inside.

"Oh, Abby, sugar." Charla enveloped her in a hug the moment she walked in the back door of the diner. "I heard about your house. You look a wreck. Go home."

Home? She had no home.

Tears bubbled up again. "I wish I'd never agreed to the makeover." Her old house hadn't been much but at least she'd had one.

"Oh, sugar, don't say that. Brady will rebuild. You'll see."

No, he wouldn't. He couldn't. Not now.

"I can't continue to impose on the Buchanons until that

happens." Not after what she'd overheard this morning. Dan didn't want her there. She was a burden. A *freebie*. And her presence caused problems for the man she was supposed to love.

"You're a mess. Go home. Get some sleep. Everything looks better after a solid eight."

"But you'll be shorthanded."

"Business is slow anyway. Everyone is still eating leftovers and recovering from hangovers. We can handle things without you." She gave Abby a little push. "With your hands shaking like that, you'd probably break every dish in the place."

Abby tried to smile. "You're the best."

"Remember that on my birthday." Charla shooed her. "Go on now."

Abby left but instead of driving to the Buchanon house, she drove to the Fairview Apartments not far from her former home on Cedar Corner. Located across the tracks on the poor side of town, Fairview was a far cry from the Buchanon home, but the tiny units were cheap, furnished and move-in ready, and she'd lived in far worse. They'd do for now.

She filled out an application, paid the deposit and after being assured by the manager than she could move in right away, drove to a day-care center near the elementary school, frustrated to find it closed for the holidays. Enrolling Lila would have to wait until tomorrow. By the time she'd finished her errands, she felt in control of her life again. And immeasurably sad.

Telling Karen of her plans proved harder than she'd expected.

"Why, Abby? Is something wrong?"

"I've imposed long enough and with the new house destroyed—" She bit her lip, fighting tears. She would not cry anymore today. Crying was useless.

"We love having you and Lila here. You can stay as long as you need."

"I've already rented an apartment and decided on a new day care for Lila." Rainbow Day Care always had openings but was not her idea of the best facility for her daughter. The cost, however, was less than she'd paid at Huckleberry and they accepted toddlers in pull-up diapers. She'd talked to them before, but now she'd do more than talk. Rainbow would work until she could find something better or until, please Lord, Lila had successful toilet training.

"This seems so sudden." Karen's frown was puzzled.

"I don't know how to thank you for all you've done. You and your family made me feel—"

"Like family?"

The pesky tears threatened. "Yes."

Karen drew her into a hug. "You *are* family, Abby."

Since coming to know the Buchanons she'd been hugged more than she had been in all her life. And she loved it. But as much as she loved living in this house, she wasn't family. Not really. Though Karen was kind to say so.

Before she forgot the very good reasons she had to leave, Abby packed her meager belongings into the car, thankful that these things had been spared, and drove away.

She was glad Lila remained at Charity's, protected from the impact of last night, but as soon as she'd unloaded her car at the apartment, the time with Charity would end, too. They had imposed enough.

When she arrived at the apartment, Brady was already there. His tall, wide body blocked the front door. Arms crossed, a scowl on his face, he demanded, "What are you doing?"

He looked wonderful and awful at the same time. His blue eyes bloodshot, fatigue hung him on him like a baggy sweatshirt. She longed to hold and comfort him the way he'd done for her last night. He'd been her rock. Without

Brady, she would have collapsed in a heap on the frozen ground.

She set the cardboard box of cleaning supplies on the concrete outside the door. "Your mother must have called you."

"She did. Did you think she'd let you move into this ratty place without asking me if I'd done something to upset you?" He uncrossed his arms and stood over her, his beloved face a mix of anger and hurt. "Have I?"

"No. No, Brady." She resisted the need to put a reassuring hand on his broad chest. "You've been wonderful."

"Then what's the deal?"

"I just thought—" She yanked in a breath, trying to decide the best thing to say. Should she admit to hearing the quarrel? Admit she knew she'd become a burden? "I'm cold out here. Can we go inside?"

He let out an exasperated huff, took the key and pushed open the door. The interior smelled stale and old. Age clung to the saggy furniture and yellowed walls.

"This is a pit. You're not staying here."

"We are. I just need to do some cleaning first."

His frown deepened as he blinked around the tiny space. "Where's Lila?"

"Still at Charity's house. I'm going after her as soon as I have the apartment ready."

"This is stupid."

"Brady, please. You'll need months, maybe longer, to rebuild my house. I can't live with your folks for a year."

"What makes you think—" The light came on behind his eyes. "You overheard Dad and me, didn't you?"

She began unloading the cleaning supplies on the single kitchen counter. The gold flecks had nearly faded away on the ancient white Formica.

"Yes."

"Okay, so you know I messed up somewhere and caused

the fire. It's my fault. My responsibility. But I'll fix it. It's what I do."

"I don't blame you." She plunked disinfectant cleaner next to the sink. "Don't think that."

"Then what? Talk to me, Abby."

"Your dad is right." She turned her back to fill the sink with water but mostly to keep from looking him in the eyes. She'd crumble if she did. "Maybe we should—step back, let things cool down for a while."

"Step back?" He came up beside her. "What are you talking about? Step back from what?"

She fanned one hand in a helpless gesture. "Every-thing."

"From the house? From each other?"

If he kept looking at her like that, she'd change her mind, and she couldn't let that happen. She owed him this much.

All she'd done was cause problems for the man she loved more than she'd believed possible. She was no good for him. If stepping away would bring peace between him and his father, and take the load off his shoulders, she loved him enough to do it.

Heart pounding in her throat with enough force to choke her, she swallowed hard and said, "Yes."

Failure ate a hole in a man. Losing Abby had gutted him.

His worst fear had happened. Because of the fire, he'd failed Abby and Lila, failed his father and the business, and he'd even failed himself.

Three days later, he still didn't understand why Abby had turned on him, but no amount of conversation seemed to shake her resolve. She used words like *needing space* and *stepping back* that all sounded like *get lost* to him.

Worse, she'd said Dad was right. Even though she claimed not to blame Brady, she did, exactly like Dad.

He'd thought she loved him. In fact, he'd been sure of

it until she'd shown him the door of her pitiful apartment. He hated seeing her live there. If he'd had his mind on his business, if he'd done his job as he should have, she wouldn't be in that situation.

He'd toyed with the idea of placing a mobile home on her property in place of the house, but Dad would go ballistic on that idea. Brady understood. They were builders. He could and would rebuild Abby's dream home. The hours might kill him, but he was determined to get Abby out of the Fairview Apartments as soon as possible. The only thing fair about the view at that place was the exit sign leading out.

With the January cold seeping into his bones, he walked along the yellow tape encircling the charred remains of Abby's house. The fire marshal had released the scene this morning. Brady still waited on the official report, but he could now begin the salvaging process. Not that there was much left to salvage.

An engine roar drew his attention to the street. His brother parked at the curb and slammed out of the Buchanon Built truck.

Hands in his coat pockets, Dawson sauntered toward him, boots padding on soil still soft from water and fire trucks. "What's up, bro?"

"Cleanup time."

"No word yet from the fire marshal?"

"None. But we both know I messed up somewhere."

"Maybe. Maybe not. Mistakes happen, Brady. Don't beat yourself up."

"Never happened to me before. I've never even had a leaky pipe."

"Yeah, well." Dawson stared around at the pile of rubble and ashes. One wobbly wall remained standing but would have to come down. "Need some help?"

"You're supposed to be on the Taylor site."

"Sawyer's there. He can handle the work for a while."

"You don't pull off jobs without a reason. What's going on?"

"I'm concerned about you. One renegade, moody brother is too many."

"Got a lot on my mind."

"What's the deal with Abby?"

He wished people would stop asking him that. "I don't know."

"Things were looking pretty sweet and then bam!" Dawson's fist hit the palm of his hand. "You're not a couple anymore."

"Yeah." Brady rubbed a hand over the back of his neck. "I guess she wasn't as serious as I'd thought."

Dawson made a rude noise in the back of his throat. "You're kidding, right? The woman's crazy in love with you. Maybe too much."

Brady frowned. "You been sniffing paint fumes or something? You're not making sense."

"I talked to her at the Buttered Biscuit."

"About me?"

"Look at it this way, Brady. Remember how reluctant she was to be part of the home makeover in the first place?"

"Yeah. But she got past that."

"Did she?"

Brady started to say yes again but stopped as the memory of her words came back to him. "She thinks nothing good ever lasts."

"Exactly. Think about her background. Her whole life has been temporary. I think she's a prime example of a self-fulfilling prophecy."

Brady rolled his eyes. "Dr. Dawson, general psychology and advice to the lovelorn. You've missed your calling, boy."

"Laugh if you want to but I'm the one Abby's talking to.

She said something about letting you go so you could get back to your life and stop worrying about her and Lila."

Brady's scowl turned to disbelief. "She didn't say that."

"She did. I think she dumped you to keep you from dumping her. As crazy and confused as that sounds, Abby thinks she's not worthy of you. I also think she backed off to protect you."

"Protect me?" His brother had a loose screw. At six-six and two-fifty, he didn't need protection. "From what?"

"Yourself. Her. Dad. She was really upset that you and Dad had fought about her house."

"She told you all this?"

"Sort of. I read between the lines."

Brady's head whirled with his brother's advice. Could Dawson be right?

His cell buzzed. Annoyed at the interruption, he yanked the device from his pocket and barked, "Buchanon."

"Mr. Buchanon, Sherry Adams with the fire investigator's office."

Brady shook himself to refocus. Getting Abby off his mind wasn't easy, but this was the call he'd been waiting for.

To Dawson, he mouthed, *Fire marshal.*

"Yes, ma'am," he said into the phone. "What have you got?"

The woman rattled off a report, but one word stood out to Brady. "Accelerant?" He glanced toward his brother, who looked every bit as stunned as he felt. "You mean someone deliberately set this fire?"

"The vandals have struck again," Dawson murmured.

After a few more moments of conversation, Brady ended the call, fuming. Between clenched teeth, he ground out, "Arson. Some worthless piece of pond scum torched Abby's house."

He should probably feel vindicated but he didn't. He was furious.

"How?" Dawson asked.

"Lacquer thinners stored in the garage. The supplier was scheduled to pick up the leftovers but hadn't yet because of the holidays. I suspected they were the cause but blamed myself for leaving them in the garage. Spontaneous combustion and all that."

"But?"

"But the fire wasn't spontaneous. The arsonist used the lacquer thinner to soak Abby's cardboard moving boxes and left a clear trail to the hot water heater."

"And all it took was a spark."

"On a night as cold as New Year's Eve, a fire was only a matter of time."

Dawson nodded thoughtfully. "The only good news in all this is that the monkey's off your back, if that makes any difference."

"It doesn't. Dad won't care. He only sees the time we've lost."

"*You've* lost. Not Dad or the business. You've kept up with the other work."

Brady rubbed a hand over his face. His nose was cold but his blood still boiled. "If I find the creep who did this—"

"Let the police do their jobs. We have enough work to do." Dawson clapped him on the shoulder. "I'm out of here. You going to call Dad about the report?"

"Later."

"What about Abby?"

Brady shook his head. "I don't know. Maybe."

Dawson's eyes, as blue as his own, studied him. "You'll think about what I said?"

Brady couldn't think of anything else.

Chapter Eighteen

Later that afternoon, Brady sat in his office at Buchanon Built Construction. At least once each day, he stopped in to check messages, go through mail Jaylee stacked on his desk and check on Quinn. Not that his brother knew his intent.

Bone weary, he rubbed a hand over the muscle aches in the back of his neck. Dawson's advice rattled around in his head along with the news of the arsonist.

The door opened and his father stepped inside. Without preamble, he held up a plastic-sleeved paper and said, "Found this in the newspaper box outside Abby's house."

Brady frowned. The newspaper box on the curb was far enough away not to burn, but he was sure it had been empty the last time he'd been to the site. "What is it?"

Dan put the sleeve on Brady's desk. "Our arsonist left a note."

Brady took up the paper and read aloud, "Are you sorry yet?" He glanced up at his father's worried face. The vandalism had escalated to a whole new level. "Sorry about what? This sounds personal, Dad."

"I thought so, too, but I've racked my brain and come up empty."

"Does Leroy know about this?"

"I'm headed over there now, but I wanted to talk to you first." Dan shifted, his work boots scrubbing the concrete. "I should have suspected the vandals from the outset instead of blaming you."

Was this an apology? From the man who was never wrong? Brady thought of a snappy comeback, an in-your-face reply, but wrestled it down. Fighting fire with fire had burned them both too many times. Today, he was too tired to fight. Tired and heartsick.

"Things happen in the heat of the moment."

"Yeah, well, sometimes you're too easy on your old man."

"Dad, could I ask you something? Man-to-man?"

Dan cocked his head, curious. Brady rarely asked for advice, particularly from his dad. "Anytime."

"If Mom left you, what would you do?"

"Go after her and do anything she wanted to get her back." Dan dragged a chair close to the desk and sat. Brady saw that he, too, was worn from the ongoing drama. Deep grooves bracketed his mouth and new lines bisected his forehead. "You're thinking about Abby?"

"I love her, Dad, and I don't know what I did wrong."

"Nothing, probably. Women are tender and Abby's had a lot of hurts. Maybe she's scared."

"That's what Dawson says."

"Yeah, well, Dawson's intuitive like his mother."

"But what do I do?"

"You and me, we're alike. We're both blockheads sometimes and can't see the forest for the trees."

"Is that supposed to make me feel better?"

Dan barked a laugh. "I've been a blockhead about Abby's house. Your mom and me, we like those two Webster girls. Miss 'em, too. That little one, she kind of eases into a man's heart. Let's get that house rebuilt."

"But you were against rebuilding. 'Give the girl the insurance money and let it go,' if I recall."

"Like I said, blockhead." He picked up the arsonist's note. "Better get this over to Leroy." He went to the door but turned back to face Brady. "First time I saw your mother, I knew she was my future. If Abby's yours, don't be a blockhead."

Moments after his father departed, Brady grabbed his work overalls from the hanger. He still didn't know what to do about Abby, but with his father's blessing, he knew what to do about her house.

The heater in her old car warmed up slowly. Abby huddled inside her coat and frowned at the silvery, overcast sky. Sleet and snow was forecast for the Texoma area. Not much, but enough to freeze pipes and make the roads slick.

She drove from the Buttered Biscuit, thoughtful. According to local gossip, Brady was working at the destroyed house. Alone. It would be dark soon. He needed to go home and rest. He was going to make himself sick.

She bit her bottom lip, guilt stricken that she'd become such a burden to him.

She wanted him to let the makeover go, to make peace with his father by forgetting about freebie Abby and her house. She would survive. She always had. She was strong and independent.

Her car bumped across the railroad tracks with a shudder. The heater finally kicked in with enough heat to clear the fog on her windshield.

As she pulled onto her street, she saw Brady's truck parked at the curb.

She parked behind him and got out, bunching her coat collar around her ears. The cold stung her eyes.

One lone man shifted through the rubble of her belongings, his russet hair and work clothes gray with soot. When he saw her, Brady straightened and lifted a hand. "Hi."

She heard the reserve in his voice and knew she'd hurt him. He didn't understand she'd done it for his well-being.

"Hi." She stood not five feet from him, every cell in her body screaming to run into his arms. He was exhausted and dirty and as steadfast as the sun. The love she bore him engulfed her in giant, rolling waves.

She closed her eyes, fighting the emotion. If she loved him enough, she'd set him free. Wasn't that a proverb or something?

She shoved her hands deep in her pockets to keep them off him, aching to wipe away the soot and worry from his face.

"Are you okay?" he asked.

She'd hurt him but he still cared enough to ask. "No. Are you?"

He stepped toward her. Broken glass crunched beneath his boot. "Be careful out here. You could get hurt."

"So could you. Give this up, Brady." *Let go of the project, so I can turn loose of this crazy, wild hope that I could ever be good enough for you.* Biting her lip, she glanced toward the neighbor's house.

"I never quit, Abby." His voice was tender. "I don't walk away. I don't let go. Don't you know that by now?"

She brought her gaze back to the beloved face. What she saw in his anguished blue eyes shook her resolve. Conviction. Concern. Love.

As steadfast as his faith, Brady had never let her down. Even though others had and even though she'd clearly hurt him, Brady, like the Lord she'd come to know through him, was still here for her.

"All I've done since we met is cause problems for you and your family."

"Not true. Problems are always around. You make them easier to bear."

She did?

"I'm in love with you, Abby. Can't you get it through your head? I need you. You need me. That's the way it's supposed to be between a man and woman. We're going through some rough times. Let's go through them together."

Knees shaking, mouth dry, she took a step. Brady took two and they were face-to-face, standing in ash and debris. His gaze searched hers, but he waited. The ball, she knew, was in her court.

"I won't ever give up, Abby. You're worth anything."

She? Awkward Abby was worth anything to big, beautiful Brady Buchanon?

Suddenly, she was no longer afraid. Not of him. Not of her past or the losses that made her shy away from commitment. Brady had proved himself over and over, and she'd been too self-focused to believe him.

"I love you, Brady. I didn't want to leave. I was just so afraid—"

"You don't have to be afraid anymore."

And she knew he spoke the truth. He'd never given her reason to distrust. Not once.

"No one ever stayed."

He grasped her upper arms, his gaze holding hers. "I will. And I need to know you'll do the same. Please. Don't leave me again."

She'd hurt him and yet he loved her. Awe swelled in her throat, choking off words. With a nod, her heart in her eyes and love about to burst from her chest, she stepped into the perfect fit of his arms. She clutched him to her, holding to what he offered. Holding to love.

There in the cold mist with dusk descending, surrounded by her broken dreams, new dreams were born.

And for the first time in her life, Abby understood what love really meant.

Epilogue

On a May evening when the purple sage was blooming
and spring was scenting the air with green and sunshine,
Abby and Lila attended a wedding on the arm of Brady
Buchanon. After more than a year of waiting, Jake Hamilton and Allison Buchanon had finally tied the knot.

"They look so in love," Abby murmured to Brady, who
sat beside her at the outdoor reception—a barbecue with
all the fixings on the grounds of Jake's ranch. Up front, at
the reception table, a photographer snapped photos of the
happy bride and groom.

Dozens ambled beneath the tent and down to the pond,
its grassy green banks mowed to golf-course perfection
for this special occasion. The wedding had been intimate,
but the reception included half the town.

"I feel weird seeing my little sister married, but it's time.
She's loved Jake since she was fourteen."

"That long?"

"When a Buchanon falls," he said, smiling into her eyes,
"he sticks."

"Is that a fact?" she asked, flirting with the man she'd
come to love and trust with all her heart.

"Mmm-hmm." He nuzzled her ear. "Fact." Below the
table he squeezed her hand.

Lila, on her opposite side, gnawed corn on the cob and basked in attention from the adored Buchanon family.

Abby could hardly believe the past six months. Amazingly, with his father's blessing and help, Brady had rebuilt her house. Because of the fire, sympathetic volunteers had turned out en masse, both to help with construction and to replace the lost furniture. Insurance, which she hadn't expected to be significant, covered much of the cost. The arsonist hadn't been caught and security cameras now guarded new construction sites.

After a month in her dream home, she was still rearranging furniture for the fun of it and adding Lila's framed angels to the walls. But the best part of the past months was Brady. She woke up each morning thanking God for this man in her life who accepted and loved her and Lila, faults and all.

"Want to take a walk down by the pond?" he asked, reaching for her empty plate.

"After eating those barbecue ribs I need to walk to Dallas!" she joked. "But this is a good start. Lila, do you want to go with us to the pond."

Across from them, the twins exchanged looks. Sawyer said, "She's still munching corn. You two lovebirds go ahead. We'll keep an eye on the princess."

Brady discarded their plates and, taking her hand, led the way across the green grass. She felt strong and secure with Brady in a way she'd never been before. She was different now. The future didn't scare her anymore. Getting close to others made her stronger, not more vulnerable.

Brady was different, too. He and his father had reached some sort of understanding. They still butted heads but eventually one of them would say, "Blockhead." They'd both laugh and walk away.

"The redbuds are gorgeous," she said, admiring the clouds of fuchsia blooms growing wild around the glassy pond.

Frogs plopped into the water with small splashes that spun out in concentric circles. Butterflies dipped and danced among the wildflowers. A dragonfly, iridescent wings green in the sunlight, buzzed overhead.

"Look at us." Brady indicated the water's mirrored reflection. Their shadowy counterparts stood side by side, hands joined. Her head came to his chin.

"We're a fit," she said.

"More than a fit, Abby." He turned toward her, eyes sincere. His voice dropped lower. "No one has ever matched me the way you do."

Her mouth curved. "I feel the same."

"It's beautiful here, isn't it?"

His change of topics puzzled her. She tilted her head. "Gorgeous."

"Do you like it? Really like it?"

She gazed around, smiling. "I love it."

"What about me? You love me, too?"

Her smile disappeared. Her breath caught. "You know I do. With all my being."

"A perfect place. A wedding. Beautiful flowers." Still holding her hand, he slipped to one knee. "The woman I want to spend the rest of my life with."

"Oh." Tears spurted at the back of her eyes. Her heart leaped, banging at her ribs.

"I love you, Abby. You're my other half, the one I've waited for. Marry me. Today, tomorrow, whenever you say. Just say you will."

"Oh. Oh." Overwhelmed, she couldn't get the words out. Finally, shaking with happiness, she managed, "I will," and fell into his arms.

She didn't care about her heels or the dress or the fact that her knees would be grass stained. All that mattered was the love of her life. She took his face in her shaking hands and stared into those beautiful eyes, eyes that someday their children might share, and when her heart could be no fuller, she kissed him.

A camera flashed. Applause and celebratory whoops broke over the pond. A voice said, "It's about time."

Abby turned in Brady's arms, surprised to find she and Brady were no longer alone. Dan held a bouncing, clapping Lila in his arms. Karen stood at his side with her daughters and sons, Sawyer, Dawson and Quinn stacked next to each other like an offensive line for the Dallas Cowboys. The bride and groom were there, too, grinning, as thrilled for Brady and Abby as for themselves.

"Mama! Bwady!" Lila reached out, wiggling her little hands. Brady swooped her into his arms, holding her between them. Abby's heart swelled with such joy and love, she thought she would burst.

Then Brady touched his forehead to Lila's and said, "What do you think, Princess? Will you be my little girl?"

Lila twisted her pretty mouth in serious thought. "Foreber?"

"Foreber and eber."

A sunny smile broke over the tiny face. She took his cheeks between her chubby hands and said with a sigh, "I thought you'd never ask."

While everyone laughed, Abby soaked up the beauty of the moment and in her heart agreed with her daughter. She and Lila and Brady, together, a family, the thing she'd been waiting for foreber.

She gazed around at the gathered group, a circle of family. Brady's family…and at long last, Abby's family, too.

* * * * *

Look for more books in New York Times
bestselling author Linda Goodnight's
THE BUCHANONS *miniseries*
on sale in 2016, wherever
Harlequin Love Inspired books and ebooks are sold!

Dear Reader,

Thank you for reading book two of The Buchanons, my series set in what is locally known as Texoma, a swath of land along the Red River that joins Texas and Oklahoma. It's a beautiful area of small towns, wooded hills and creeks, and friendly people.

Christmas is wonderful anywhere, but small-town parades and festivals have a warmth and flavor all their own. I hope you enjoyed sharing Christmas with Abby, Brady and all the Buchanons.

I love hearing from readers. You may contact me through my website: www.lindagoodnight.com. From there, you can also sign up for my quarterly newsletter and connect with me on social media. If you prefer, you may write to me c/o Love Inspired, 233 Broadway, Suite 1001, New York, NY 10279.

Merry Christmas,

Linda Goodnight

COMING NEXT MONTH FROM
Love Inspired®

Available November 17, 2015

A RANGER FOR THE HOLIDAYS
Lone Star Cowboy League • by Allie Pleiter

Ranger Finn Brannigan wakes up in a hospital with no clue who he is. But this Christmas, with philanthropist Amelia Klondike by his side, he'll recover more than his memory—he'll find a love to last a lifetime.

AN AMISH NOEL
The Amish Bachelors • by Patricia Davids

Emma Swartzentruber has been content keeping house for her widowed father—until he announces she must marry. When former love Luke Bowman is hired to revitalize her family business for the holidays, could it be her chance at happily-ever-after?

GIFT-WRAPPED FAMILY
Family Ties • by Lois Richer

Widow Mia Granger is shocked to hear lawyer Caleb Grant say she owns a ranch—and has a stepdaughter. With his support, her bond with Lily grows and Mia realizes opening her heart could mean a new family this Christmas.

THE DOCTOR'S CHRISTMAS WISH
Village Green • by Renee Ryan

When Keely O'Toole becomes guardian to her seven-year-old cousin, she'll look next door to Dr. Ethan Scott for advice. Can the joy of the holidays and one little girl turn these dueling neighbors into husband and wife?

HOLIDAY HOMECOMING
The Donnelly Brothers • by Jean C. Gordon

Former television reporter Natalie Delacroix returns home to be with her family and take a break from her fast-paced life. Instead, she finds herself producing a Christmas Eve pageant and envisioning a future with her high school sweetheart, Pastor Connor Donnelly.

SECOND CHANCE CHRISTMAS
The Rancher's Daughters • by Pamela Tracy

Years ago, a painful tragedy made Elise Hubrecht run from her hometown—and her boyfriend, Cooper Smith. Now that she's back on her father's ranch, could this holiday season be Cooper's new chance with the girl who got away?

LICNM1115

REQUEST YOUR FREE BOOKS!

2 FREE INSPIRATIONAL NOVELS
PLUS 2
FREE
MYSTERY GIFTS

Love Inspired®

SPECIAL EXCERPT FROM

Love Inspired®

*Amelia Klondike promises to help amnesiac
Finn Brannigan get his memory back. But can they
also give themselves a merry Christmas?*

*Read on for a sneak preview of
A RANGER FOR THE HOLIDAYS,
the next book in the Love Inspired continuity*
LONE STAR COWBOY LEAGUE

.

"Everything has changed, hasn't it?"

Finn heard the same catch in her tone that he felt in his own chest. He knew he was Finn Brannigan, but didn't know if that was good news. The sense that the life he'd forgotten wasn't a happy one still pressed against him.

"So it's just your name? That's all you remember?"

"And my age." *Tell her you're a Ranger*, the honorable side of him scolded the other part that foolishly refused to confess. It felt as though everything would slam back into place once tomorrow dawned, so would it be terrible to just keep this one night as the happy victory it was? She'd be perfectly entitled to refuse his friendship once all the facts came to light.

Amelia laid her hand on his arm and he felt that connection he had each time she touched him. As if she needed him, even though it was the other way around. "I can't imagine what you must be feeling right now."

The return of his memory was a double-edged sword. "There's a lot floating out there—fuzzy impressions I can't quite get a fix on, but…I can't tell you what it means to know my whole name." He hesitated for a moment before admitting, "For a while I was terrified it wouldn't come back. That I'd end up one of those freak stories you read about in supermarket tabloids."

She laughed. "I can't imagine that. You're far too normal."

Normal? Nothing about him felt normal. The scary part was the constant sense that his normal wasn't anywhere near as nice as right now was, sitting out under the stars near a roaring fire hearing…

Christmas carols. A group of high school students began to sing "Away in a Manger." Finn felt his stomach tighten.

He waited for his unnamed aversion to all things Christmas to wash over him. It came, but more softly. More like regret than flat-out hate. Finn closed his eyes and tried to hear it the way Amelia did, reverent and quiet instead of slow and mournful. Why couldn't he grasp the big dark thing lurking just out of his reach? What made him react to Christmas the way he did?

Don't miss
A RANGER FOR THE HOLIDAYS
by Allie Pleiter, available December 2015 wherever
Love Inspired® books and ebooks are sold.